1632 & Beyond Issue #5

1632 and Beyond, Virginia DeMarce,
Natalie Silk, George Grant, Marc Tyrrell,
Bob Finegold, Iver P. Cooper

Flint's Shards, Inc.

ERIC FLINT'S 1632 & BEYOND ISSUE #5

Editor-in-Chief Bjorn Hasseler
Editor Bethanne Kim
Editor Chuck Thompson
Cover Artwork by Garrett W. Vance
Art Director Garrett W. Vance

1. Science Fiction-Alternate History
2. Science Fiction-Time Travel

eBook ISBN: 978-1-962398-08-4
Paperback ISBN: 978-1-962398-09-1

Distributed by Flint's Shards Inc.
339 Heyward Street, #200
Columbia, SC 29201

Key Points: Assiti Shards Timeline

April 2, 2000 - Grantville, West Virginia disappeared in the Ring of Fire. It is transported to May 25, 1631, Thuringia, the Germanies.

"Dozens" of events that resulted in nothing more than sea monster sightings, *Time Spike*, location 38/937.

2007 - The Alexander Correction Center disappears from Illinois. The Quiver stutters through the past, also collecting Cherokee and soldiers on the Trail of Tears, Spanish conquistadors, and Native Americans from at least two earlier time periods before depositing all of them in the Cretaceous Era.

November, 2008 - A shard takes a squad of ROTC cadets from Fort Dix, New Jersey. It moves them only a few miles, but to December 21, 1776. *The Crossing* was published fourth, but is the third major Assiti shard chronologically.

Shortly into our future - The cruise ship *Queen of the Sea* is transported from the Caribbean Sea to the Mediterranean Sea, September 15, 321 BC.

Sometime after that - A big rig hauling a fuel tanker, a pickup, and part of a convenience store are moved to the vicinity of Cahokia, Illinois in 1005 AD.

Other 1632 Universe Publications

1632 by Eric Flint created the 1632 universe and the Assiti Shards. Free download available at Baen.com/1632.html.

Short-List of Titles to Jump into the Series:

Ring of Fire anthology edited by Eric Flint

1633 by Eric Flint and David Weber

1634: The Baltic War by Eric Flint and David Weber

All books available through Baen.com, booksellers, and used bookstores.

Also Available:

Grantville Gazette Volumes 1 – 102, magazine edited by Eric Flint, Paula Goodlett, Walt Boyes, Bjorn Hasseler. Available on 1632Magazine.com.

1632 Universe novels and "Eric Flint, Ring of Fire Series" on Baen.com

Recently Released and Forthcoming:

The 1st of odd numbered months: New issues of Eric Flint's 1632 & Beyond.

See the "News and New Books" section at the end of this publication.

Ongoing: Baen is re-releasing select 1632 books originally released by Eric Flint's Ring of Fire Press, starting with Bjorn Hasseler's NESS books. Please check the Baen.com e-arc bundles and new releases regularly!

Contents

News and New Books

Available Now and Coming Soon

Introduction to Issue 5

The Magdeburg Messenger
(1632 Fiction)

V elma Hardesty first appeared in *Grantville Gazette* 4. Virginia De-Marce concludes this character's arc in "A Rose By Any Other Song." This story also includes Shakespeare's grandsons.

Natalie Silk continues the story of Rahel and the village of Zaborstadt in "Down This Path."

Have you ever set something aside and completely forgotten about it? It happens, in George Grant's "Mail From Up-Time."

George Grant also provides our first flash fiction, with "The Small Crisis."

Marc Tyrrell explains another step in the process of how military intelligence got from the first days after the Ring of Fire to what we see later in the series, with "Making Hay While the Sun Shines."

"Among the Faithful" is Robert Finegold's story about the Committees of Correspondence during Krystalnacht, but told from the perspective of townspeople in the Rhineland.

State Library Papers
(1632 Non-Fiction)

Iver P. Cooper explains beekeeping and its possibilities in the 1632 universe.

Editor's Notes

Several of us attended the Fantasci convention in Durham, North Carolina. We will have more to say later. For now, rest assured that the future of 1632 and the Assiti Shards is looking very good.

Magdeburg Messenger
1632 Fiction

Flint's Shards, Inc.

A Rose By Any Other Song
Virginia DeMarce

Grantville, SoTF
September 1635

"And now, we bring you *News from the Netherlands*."

The general manager of the Voice of America pondered as he listened.

"It's a good skit." The VOA disk jockey grinned.

"Tom and Dick Quiney are, if nothing else, reliably irreverent," John Grover admitted. He was facing a move to Bamberg as a result of the last election and was having a bit of trouble watching his first baby radio station grow up.

"Not always kind, though," Jennifer Sonderman observed.

"Satire isn't meant to be kind."

"I don't like the music they picked for the background, though," Marc Kronzburg said. He was the sales manager, responsible for bringing in the station's advertising and, therefore, its income. Which meant that he had a sharp sense of what would appeal to listeners.

"*Es ist ein Ros' entsprungen* is very popular," the disk jockey said. "The name, 'Rose,' is right. It works if you sing it in English, too." He whistled and then sang in a baritone that would never make it onto the air, "A little Rose has sprung up, or sprouted." Then he nodded. "I've heard up-timers call a baby a 'sprout,' so it's the same as the German."

"But Velma Hardesty is an up-timer," Kronzburg objected. "I want something up-time. Plus, *Es ist ein Ros'* is well-known, but it's not exactly zippy. Let me ask around and see what I can find. This can be broadcast on Thursday just as well as on Tuesday. It will still be topical."

The Old Folks Band suggested "Rose of San Antone." That didn't seem quite right, given the title of the skit, since Velma Hardesty's new husband, the portly merchant who had begotten the infant Rose in question, was Dutch; not from Texas.

Benny Pierce offered "Rambling Rose."

"No, that's not right, either," the second disk jockey said. "Babies don't ramble. My cousin has three. I assure you that they eat, burp, sleep, urp, and fill their diapers. Then they eat again. Rinse and repeat. Literally, as far as the diapers are concerned. They don't ramble."

"At least they picked a name that it's easy to find music for. It's not as if they named the kid Erdmuthe or Mechthilde."

"Just a minute," Errol Mercer said the next day when he came in with his wife Lisbet's band for the dance program. "Velma Hardesty moved up to the Netherlands, didn't she? To where that man she married is from? Is that what you're talking about?"

The disk jockey winced. Errol was a nice guy, but he tended to be a bit oblivious to anything that wasn't set to a melody and didn't require instrumental arrangement.

"Yeah, they're living there." He sighed. "The place was in the paper when they got married last fall. You must have missed it."

"Probably," Errol answered, utterly undismayed. "There's just something that's tickling the back of my mind, from before the Ring of Fire, when I was playing with that Golden Oldies band over in Fairmont." He turned to Lisbet. "Look that place up, would you, Lisbet? Can you go down to the paper and pull the back issues for November, okay?"

"Got it," Errol cackled with triumph as he ran into the VOA office a couple of hours later. "Got it in one. And that Fernando, the king up there, he's Spanish, isn't he?"

"Sure, but they aren't calling it the Spanish Netherlands and the United Netherlands separately, any more. It's just 'The Netherlands' or 'The Low Countries' now. He's 'king in the Low Countries.'"

"Close enough for government work, and if you ask me, VOA is part of the government. Lisbet, call a rehearsal, will you. We've got to rehearse this before the variety hour goes on the air."

Which meant that, by the time all the band members got there, they had exactly forty-five minutes to rehearse.

"And now," the announcer proclaimed, "*Grantville Gossip with the Quiney Brothers.* 'All the things you want to know about all the people you sorta wish you didn't.' Featuring, today, *News from the Netherlands.*"

"Ladies and gentlemen in the radio audience. Just in from the Netherlands, Velma Hardesty had another baby. At her age! We may have lost count, but this one is probably Number Five, if not Number Six. It's a girl and they've named her..."

Lisbet's dance band rolled in with, "There is a Rose in Spanish Haarlem..."

November 1636

"I know Velma Hardesty was something of a joke"—Errol Mercer waved down Cora for another cup of coffee—"but this isn't something you can make funny. She died up north there, in the Netherlands, having another baby. She's dead, man. Like, I mean, a corpse. 'The worms crawl in; the worms crawl out; the worms play pinochle on her snout.' Even if she wasn't a very good mother—even if she was an absolutely horrible mother—you still don't want to hurt Pam's feelings. She was a few years behind me in school, but she was a nice kid. So are Cory Joe and Susan—nice kids, that is."

"What did she name this one? Dahlia? Camellia? Astilbe? Zinnia?" Benny Pierce grinned. "Artemisia, like that painter lady?"

"It's a boy," Gary Haggerty said. "They named him Laurent, for her husband. Laurent Jacques Pierre Mauger. The 'Jacques Pierre' is for Dumais who worked for us Garbage Guys for a while. He took out citizenship, just before Mayor Dreeson was assassinated, if I remember rightly. He's one of those Huguenots, like Mauger, and went back to the Netherlands with him for a job managing his new lava lamp startup company, but he's kept his citizenship here. I hear from him every now and then."

"So how do you think the VOA should handle it?" Sebastian Fleck asked. John and Leota Grover's foster son, just a kid when he had showed up in Grantville, was a senior in high school already as well as a part-time disk jockey.

Errol tilted his chair back on its hind legs. "Just give a straightforward obit. Nothing fancy, no editorials, no comments, no skits. Born. Died. Preceded in death by daughter Tina. Survived by husband and five kids.

Mention who the older kids married if you want to add a flourish, but that's it."

Cora Ennis herself plopped a cup of coffee, milk, no sugar, down in front of Errol and looked across at the senior VOA man. "Don't let the Quiney brothers go into who the fathers of the various kids were or might have been."

He raised his eyebrows.

"Just don't, or I'll skin you alive."

"Tom Quiney isn't writing for the VOA right now," Sebastian answered, even though Cora had been speaking to Aubrey Weldon. The Londoner, who had wandered into Grantville largely because one of his old school friends was already here and working as a researcher at the state library, had taken over quite a bit of the English-language program planning.

Well, really, most of it. There were only so many up-timers to go around; fewer of them in Grantville every year. Hardly any of them wanting to work for what the VOA could pay.

"Master Massinger is getting ready to put on some kind of big production in Magdeburg, so everyone's way too busy," Aubrey explained. "I haven't had any short pieces from Tom since late last summer. Early fall, maybe. They were having cash flow problems for a while after Mistress Antonia died, so I got several, but now, with Massinger back in charge..."

France, April 1637

"You did very well in extricating Milkau from the hands of his blackmailers." Benjamin de Rohan, duke of Soubise, nodded.

"Thank you, Your Grace." Joachim Sandrart bowed. "I am hoping that my father-in-law will be more prudent from now on. He...has an eye for opportunities to make money rapidly. Even if some aspects of them are...chancy."

"You were tactful."

Sandrart bowed again.

"Would you be interested in a short trip to Burgundy by way of Paris? I need to send some information to my brother that I do not wish to entrust to written form. Partly in regard to the...preliminary overtures...in regard to...ah, sensitive matters, but I need to consult with our sister Anne first. We must return to the days of Homer, when the message was carried in the mind of the messenger, I think."

Sandrart swallowed. "I would be most honored to accept such a commission. I have, however, made several commitments in the Netherlands to complete paintings. For example, M. Laurent Mauger of Haarlem wants a full family portrait with all his children, their spouses, and his sisters. Then he also wants one of his two youngest children, the ones by his late wife, the up-timer. One which will include a post-mortem portrait of her." He cleared his throat. "As an angel, watching over them from the realms above. Surrounded by a frame of roses climbing on a trellis. The motif is sadly papist. A good Calvinist can scarcely endorse it. But he has provided me with a generous advance."

"Then...you cannot comply with my request?" Soubise stood up.

Sandrart, taking this as a dismissal, bowed again, preparing to back out of the room. "Ah, no. Not as stated."

"Wait."

Sandrart waited.

Soubise turned his back, looking out the window. "Can you delay those?"

"Not for long."

"For long enough?"

"I think so." Sandrart looked at his noble patron's back. "Or, I could try to complete them by mid-June and then join you in Paris, going on to Burgundy afterwards. But... My marriage with Johanna is going well. Very well, I think. Still, we have not been married long, and she is young. I, ah, don't think that she will like it at all if I'm away a lot longer than I said I would be."

Soubise turned. Smiling. "So, then. Write to her explaining my request, and we will find out very soon whether or not you have what it takes to enter a career in the higher levels of the diplomatic service as a good man lying abroad in the service of his country. *Certainement!*"

He moved across the room and accompanied Sandrart to the head of the stairs, where he automatically paused. Paused, because protocol prescribed that the host should at least make it appear as if he were considering accompanying his guest down the stairs. Automatically, because he had first been assigned to read the protocol manuals back when he was cutting his second teeth. He no longer thought about these things.

"Have you ever met Leopold Cavriani?"

"It has not been my pleasure."

"Perhaps you will have a chance to do so. Complete your paintings with my best wishes, young man, and as soon as you are done, rejoin me in France. After Burgundy, be prepared to continue on to Grantville, if necessary." He winked. "By way of Frankfurt am Main, if needs be for the tranquility of your matrimonial situation. Cavriani will find a way to send you more detailed instructions."

Haarlem, Netherlands
May/June 1637

Sandrart, after having submitted several sketches of possible arrangements on the basis of Laurent Mauger's descriptions of the number, connections, and individual sizes of his various kinfolk, had finally managed to get them all together.

Mauger, the centerpiece of the proposed group portrait, was currently represented by an ornate chair and a rather large bolster propped up against it.

Mauger, the portly merchant, was standing next to the artist.

"I insist," his older son, Barendt, was saying through tight lips, "that if this is to be a family portrait, the one that Tengnagel did of Mama must be painted into it, next to you."

Laurent did not particularly like the portrait that Tengnagel had done of Adriaantje Kleelinck.

He had not, in fact, particularly liked Adriaantje, but he had always done his duty conscientiously toward the only child, the heiress, who had been such an advantageous alliance for the Mauger firm. Of the nine children to whom she had given birth, only Barendt, now twenty-four years old, and Jan Willem, who had just turned twenty, survived.

The two adult sons, standing directly behind Mauger's chair, would be flanked by Laurent's array of five unmarried, middle-aged sisters and half-sisters.

Sandrart frowned, considering. The unbalanced number of available sisters would lead to an unbalanced composition. The portrait would not include Marie and Aeltje, who had married, or Louise, now deceased, who had also married. His mouth quirked. Including the full panoply of Mauger's sisters' descendants would require something the size of the depictions of municipal militias that city fathers commissioned for their town halls. Or a civic association. Or a city council itself.

Perhaps a somewhat more modern arrangement than the traditional symmetry of family portraits, a deliberately unbalanced design...

He made a suggestion.

The adult sons kept glowering.

Mauger kept talking.

He would like to have Rose and little Laurent on his lap—a nice tribute to the importance of fatherly affection.

If Adriaantje's portrait was to be on an easel on one side of his chair, then there must be a portrait of Velma painted into this one also.

The adult members of the Mauger family glowered even harder, united for once in their loathing of the late Velma Hardesty.

Even Mauger realized that this idea was not being well-received.

"Two separate portraits, perhaps?" Sandrart said tentatively.

"No," Mauger answered with his usual stubbornness. "One." He glowered back at his sons and sisters.

Then, suddenly, he beamed.

"No, maybe two. But not just two portraits. I shall..." He stopped for a moment. "I shall sponsor a monument for my Velma, one that will cause her to be remembered in history. Like that painting in Rudolstadt that depicts Countess Katharina the Heroic defying the Duke of Alba."

Sandrart could not, at the moment, recall any particularly heroic actions that anyone had attributed to Velma Hardesty.

"A portrait," Mauger continued, "but not just a portrait. I shall sponsor a trilogy of plays about great heroines who led resistance to tyranny. After all, my late wife was cousin to Michael Stearns himself, so it is only appropriate, don't you think?"

Sandrart swallowed.

"Not just performances. New plays. Or new productions, at the very least. With sets that have, in the background, large canvases that show my Velma as... Well, as whichever woman is the heroine in that particular play."

As they considered the cost of this, Mauger's relatives frowned even harder.

"There should be some association with Grantville. I'll hire Philip Massinger's troupe to put the trilogy on and have the series open in Grantville before taking it to Magdeburg and then bring it here to the Netherlands for a 'triumphal tour.' What do you think?"

"Massinger's troupe may not be in Grantville, right now. They went to Hesse early this year, at the invitation of Landgrave Philipp of Hesse-Butzbach. They've been doing repertoire out of his palace while things in Grantville calm down. Some of Tom Quiney's satire got a little too pointed to please the up-timers, even if he is a grandson of the famous William Shakespeare."

Laurent Mauger stroked his beard. "Plays to honor my adored Velma, written by William Shakespeare's grandson."

His oldest son turned around and slammed out of the room, ruining the pose that Sandrart had been sketching onto the canvas. His brother followed him, ruining the entire composition.

* * *

Sandrart still did not have the pleasure of making the acquaintance of Leopold Cavriani, but the man's son Marc arrived from Magdeburg with instructions in regard to various projects of interest to Huguenots.

Jacques Pierre Dumais suggested that as a tribute to the dukes of Rohan and Soubise, the first play of the trilogy honoring Velma should be a completely new production of a screenplay that their late mother had written.

Mauger agreed. "However, I will commission entirely new plays for the second and third parts of the trilogy."

Grantville, July 1637

"Catherine de Parthenay's *Judith* has not previously been staged, to the best of my knowledge," Shackerly Marmion said. "Certainly not in public. There may have been private readings."

Mauger's project was causing a lot of discussion among the members of the theatrical community in Grantville.

"I hadn't realized the guy was actually *that* rich," Lorrie Mundell said. "Rich enough to afford all this, I mean. When he was in town a couple of years ago, he just seemed to be a fairly well-to-do wine merchant. Rich enough to fascinate Velma, obviously, but that didn't take a lot, given the string of losers she slept with all her life."

"Well, actually, he is. At least, I guess he is. He's signed all these contracts."

Dick Quiney picked up his clipboard. "What do we know about the duke of Rohan's mother? Where can we find out more?"

"Do we even need to?" Christina Pittlin asked with her usual practicality. "We can get enough out of the encyclopedia to put a bio on the programs we distribute. Get someone to draw a sketch of her standing next to King Henri II of France while he was signing the Edict of Nantes and stick that up the nose of Monsieur Gaston. What we really need right now is a complete copy of the screenplay, which we do *not* have. Where are we going to get one?"

"Somebody get onto the radio with Carey Calagna in Besançon. The duke of Rohan should have a copy, if anybody does."

"I've seen Signora Gentileschi's painting—one of them; she's done several on the theme. Which particular villain should the program notes hint that Holofernes is standing in for, this time around?"

Johann Georg Hardegg cleared his throat. "As a lawyer, I'm about as far from specializing in these new laws that the up-timers have introduced, copyright, trademarks, 'intellectual property,' as they say, as a lawyer can be. I rather feel that I should tell you, though, that if you plan to use Signora Gentileschi's paintings of these events as in any way a *direct* inspiration for your backdrops, rather than composing new versions, it may, might...will...be prudent for you to investigate whether or not she will have a claim to some sort of royalties."

"The cost, the cost," Massinger moaned.

They couldn't afford the rights to use copies of Signora Gentileschi's painting.

"In any case, Mauger wants a new painting anyway, one that will be of 'museum quality' but can also be reproduced as an advertising poster," Marc said. "With Velma depicted as Judith. He's already signed a contract with Joachim Sandrart, who is in France with Soubise at the moment, but should hit Grantville by late summer or early fall."

"None of this is going to come cheap."

"I have every expectation that the man is going to bankrupt himself," Massinger answered. "As long as we are paid before he completes the process, then, as the Poles say, 'not my circus; not my monkeys.' It's a real coup for Tom and Dick Quiney to be writing the second and third plays."

* * *

"Tom can manage two scripts in short order," Dick Quiney said. "He may crib a bit here and there, but it can be done. However, we do need to know what you want him to write a play about. Or what M. Mauger wants us to write a play about."

"A heroine of the resistance against tyranny."

"Hah," Shackerly Marmion said. "What about Gretchen Richter?"

"No!" Massinger exploded. "Never. For one thing, she's no Calvinist, and a Huguenot is paying for this."

"So what are the themes?" Dick asked again. He could be tenacious when it came to keeping the production schedule on track.

Massinger considered. "Well, with Judith as the heroine of the first of the trilogy, it is clear that the second one should be Jael and Sisera. There's no decent existing play on that theme—at least no full-length music drama. Mauger has decided he wants to build up—straight drama for the first, since that is the way it was written; drama with music for the second. So it will be something of a triumph for Tom to write something entirely new."

A triumph, Dick thought, *if the play succeeds, But also a lot more work.*

"Who's going to compose the new music?"

"I don't think it's been decided yet."

"Signora Gentileschi has also painted Jael and Sisera, you know."

"We won't be able to get rights to or afford royalties on that one, either. It's going to be 'Art by Sandrart' from beginning to end—concept work, backdrops, posters, the whole thing. Velma included."

"Sandrart's really a diplomat, you know. What if his day job hauls him away in the middle of this project?"

"Right now, Mauger is paying him enough to make launching the trilogy his day job."

"Will Tom have the time to do both of the new plays, or will you have to bring in another playwright to finish Mauger's commission on time?" Shackerley Marmion asked Massinger hopefully. Teaching at the high school didn't pay remarkably well. "For that matter, what's the theme of the third one?"

"We've thought about Susanna and the Elders as one possibility. After all, Gentileschi did a painting of that, too."

"I like that," Marmion said. "I'm even enthusiastic, since it would give an opportunity to depict female nudity, or near enough. Also, it would neatly make all the heroines biblical—or, well, at least apocryphal."

Massinger cleared his throat. "Tom will have time to write it. There will be no nudity onstage. Or even near nudity onstage. This trilogy is a serious memorial to a grieving husband's deceased wife. A grieving Calvinist husband."

"From what the gossip was, back when he married her," Lorrie Mundell contributed, "Laurent Mauger seriously appreciated Velma's nudity. A lot."

"While, for my part, I seriously doubt," Marmion said, "that Judith, Jael, and Susannah were Calvinists any more than Gretchen Richter is."

"That point is not likely to occur to Laurent Mauger."

Marmion backed off and sulked.

Grantville, September 1637

"What about tying the trilogy together with a little 'play within a play' theme?" Tom asked Dick. "Carey Calagna did get a copy of the screenplay from the duke and sent it to Grantville by special courier. What about Catherine de Parthenay herself? She's something of a heroine of the resistance, considering that her first husband had been killed in 1572 in the St. Bartholomew's massacre, and she had withstood two sieges of La Rochelle before her death in 1631. Plus, it would be a tribute to Rohan. We could introduce each of the plays with a very short act, a *vignette*, on her life."

"Would the duke object to having his mother portrayed on stage?"

Massinger radioed a query to Mauger in Haarlem.

Mauger replied that he would obtain permission—in fact, he would see to it himself. In practice, this meant that Jacques-Pierre Dumais meandered off to speak to Soubise in France, given that Rohan was temporarily absent from Besançon on vague "diplomatic duties" for which Grand Duke Bernhard needed him. Permission granted.

Then Dumais meandered into Grantville, in company with Marc Cavriani.

Who was extraordinarily surprised to find Susannah Allegretti there as a guest of his sister Idelette, who had considerable fun tweaking her brother's nose.

Tom Quiney, just then, was too busy to care. "Since Rohan's daughter just got married this year, we should put a pair of young lovers in the *vignette* for the third play. Even if Catherine de Parthenay in the real world didn't live long enough to attend the wedding."

"As a tribute to Mauger and Velma," Christina Pittlin suggested, "you should have the young heroine named 'Rose.'"

"Rohan's daughter," Massinger pointed out, "is named Marguerite. Shouldn't she be the heroine?"

"Rose can be a lady-in-waiting to the mature Catherine. Ladies-in-waiting are always handy, when it comes to plays. Every great lady has a few. That way we won't have to waste time getting permission to show Marguerite onstage. Rohan agreed to a dead mother, but he might not be so compliant when it comes to a living daughter. The wedding can be taking place offstage."

Sandrart adapted the mature Catherine de Parthenay from her actual portrait. For the first vignette, in which the tragically widowed eighteen-year-old Catherine married the *vicomte* de Rohan, he had used his imagination a bit. Quite a bit. And as for the *vicomte*?

"Why shouldn't I have used Dumais for the model?" he asked Marmion rhetorically. It had to be rhetorical, since the posters were already being printed. "The man *is* gorgeous; the actor playing the role won't look anywhere near that good, but *comme ci, comme ça*."

"After all," Massinger said, "casts change. The point of the posters is to bring in the paying audience."

By the time they were preparing materials for the third play, everyone was tired. Sandrart at first proposed to use his wife Johanna as a model for the idealized Rose, but his father-in-law balked at the idea. He would need another model. None of the actresses in Massinger's troupe was quite right. But...

Yes, Marc Cavriani and Susanna Allegretti did quite well.

Leopold Cavriani was privately amused at the portrayal of his quite Catholic potential daughter-in-law as a Huguenot heroine. Or, at least, lady-in-waiting to a Huguenot heroine.

Massinger sighed. "Mauger wants even more music in the final play of the trilogy. And a ballet. He doesn't exactly want an opera, but it's getting perilously close. We're going to have to hire more musicians, or borrow some, from somewhere. Does anybody know where Gabriel Möhlich has gone? I need a ballet master, and I need one right now if Mauger expects me to get all this onstage by Christmas!"

"My father is selling property to finance this," Barendt Mauger wrote to Dumais. "Selling real estate. He's disposing of profitable, long-term, investments. If the annuities settled on my aunts were not firmly in trusts, he would be looting them. He's running the family bankrupt. This is insane."

Dumais showed the letter to Leopold Cavriani.

He and Marc set off for Haarlem again.

Susanna Allegretti watched them go, her invitation to join the court of the new Grand Duchess of Tuscany in Florence in her hand.

Haarlem, Netherlands
January 1638

"It was a sudden, massive, heart attack," Dumais wrote to the dukes of Rohan and Soubise. "In spite of the high level of conflict within the Mauger family, I have no doubt that it was natural. For these past few months, especially these most recent weeks, Laurent had been as a man possessed, desperate to see his monumental tribute to Madame Hardesty brought to fruition. He gloried in the reports of the trilogy's success in Grantville. He sold even more and transferred funds to ensure that it will be staged in Magdeburg this spring.

"He had not lost his mind, no. He knew what he wanted to do. The fund transfers are irrevocable; Barendt and Jan Willem will not be able to claw them back. The annuities for the ladies, for Laurent's unmarried sisters, are still secure. The full dowries for his married sisters were paid long ago. However..."

Barendt and Jan Willem would otherwise be building up the Mauger family fortune from scratch.

Laurent Mauger had not really been *that* rich, as Lorrie Mundell had phrased it.

Barendt and Jan Willem refused to accept any responsibility for their half-siblings. They repudiated them. Refused to acknowledge the validity of the Grantville marriage. Called upon the agreement according to which their father had promised not to remarry. Hired lawyers.

Dumais radioed to Magdeburg, letting Leopold Cavriani know that he, himself, had the little children and intended to bring them to Magdeburg and put them under the care of their half-brother Cory Joe Lang and, by extension, the USE government.

"Don't leave, yet," Cavriani answered. "Cory Joe Lang and his wife are in Prague."

"Isn't there a sister?"

"Two sisters. Susan is wealthy, now, because of the Barbies; legally emancipated. But, still, very young. Perhaps not even twenty years old, quite? The time changes from up-time to down-time cause confusion when it comes to the exact, precise, legally important ages of the up-timers; not just from the Julian calendar to the Gregorian, but there is the lack of synchronicity between April of 2000 and May of 1631 that gives a second sequence of 'lost days.' The children's other maternal half-sister is in Leiden. She is a librarian."

Dumais considered that to be an unsatisfactory solution. Leiden, obviously, was in the Netherlands, where the lawyers for the other Maugers could do dastardly legal things to the little ones, Rose and Laurent. Yes, Pam Hardesty and her husband, Jean Louis LaChapelle were there, but he was only a student of science at the university. Not in a position of power, even though he was a Huguenot.

Huguenot.

Dumais stood there, looking down at the sleeping children.

The thought of his own patron, Henri duc de Rohan, head of the Huguenot movement, as the guardian of these helpless children struck him as...well...ideal. Given that the monument to Velma that had destroyed their father had also, unquestionably, raised the current level of...visibility...of the duke on the international scene. By quite a lot, really.

Little Laurent slept on.

Rose opened her eyes and looked at him.

Down This Path
Natalie Silk

R ahel used the apron she wore to wipe the stubborn bits of dough and flour from her hands while she walked to the door. She had an idea who was on the other side just by the loud and incessant banging. Netanel almost hit her forehead just as she opened the door. They both gasped at the same time in surprise.

"Herr Netanel, good day! Has your wife borne you the baby?" She felt momentarily uncomfortable when he looked at her bare head and arched his left brow. He quickly composed himself. She disliked having to wear a cap all the time and didn't see any reason to wear one in her own home—especially when she was alone. Even when her father was in his shop behind their home, cobbling shoes.

"Sarah is still in the pains of childbirth."

"Oh." She couldn't think of anything better to say.

"Your mother asks that you bring the medicine in the basket that she forgot in her haste. She tells me you know where it would be."

"Of course. Wait here." She grabbed the latch of the door, but Netanel used his right hand to brace it from fully closing. She wondered why he did this.

"I leave you. Beryl asked that I go to wait with her husband."

Rahel watched him walk away and closed the door when he was no longer in view, allowing herself a shake of the head and a giggle. The message was a code that if Netanel got underfoot, he would be sent to her. She recalled all the times she was bored during services and would peek through the curtains that separated the men and women to watch how enthusiastically Netanel would *daven*. His swaying and bowing were so deep and fast. It was no surprise to her, as she imagined him making a nuisance of himself by asking question after question, flitting around his wife's bedside and just getting in the way of her mother and his mother-in-law, Beryl. Being a first-time father—hopefully of a son—exacerbated his nervous energy. That his mother-in-law had persuaded him to go to her husband was a feat in and of itself. At least it was a blessing the baby would arrive during a clear and calm spring day.

Rahel had overheard her mother saying to a friend that no one, at least in their village, knew of any man who wanted to witness a birth. Jewish men would pray outside of the home or in a separate room until the baby was cleaned and swaddled.

Her mother, Rhea, was the midwife in their small town, Zaborstadt, which was at least a day's travel north of Grantville and a mile away from Jena. In fact, Rhea was so well respected, that she helped women outside of the synagogue.

Rahel rolled the dough in a ball and covered it with a cloth, washed her hands, and untied and flung her apron on the table. She grabbed the basket of "medicine" on the way to the door. It was actually two apples, cheese, and bread that was almost stale. She was about to step through the door but stopped with a huff—she had almost forgotten. She put the basket down and put her hair up, looking around for her cap. Hair properly covered, Rahel secured the door and went around the back to Papa's workshop to tell him that she was called to Sarah's home.

She started down the road, glad that her monotonous day was interrupted. She soon passed the path, now overgrown, that she and Yechezqel, the youngest of her five brothers and her co-conspirator, took to their special place by the Saale River. She sighed from one such memory.

* * *

Rahel had almost bumped into Yechezqel when he suddenly stopped on the path to their special place. "Why stop?" She looked up at him in surprise. "The rabbi isn't here today."

"I was only being cautious. Put the blanket over there." He pointed to a patch of tall grass.

"I know. It's the same place."

She unfolded and fluffed the old, patched blanket on the grass and then sat down on it, patiently waiting for her brother to cast and then secure his fishing rod in a hole with stones to brace it. She thought he was clever. He told her the first time they "went fishing" together that it didn't matter whether he caught anything. What was important was the rule he was helping his only sister to break.

Yechezqel put his tackle basket down on the edge of the blanket before sitting next to her, then retrieved an old, battered slate that each brother in turn used to learn how to read. As in other times, they sat side by side, her brother writing words and saying them out loud while Rahel traced the letters with her index finger, repeating what he said and wrote. This was the rule they were breaking. It wasn't important for Rahel, a girl, to know how to read and write: she was supposed to know how to keep a proper home and raise her husband's children correctly.

The images of them sitting and reading faded. She sighed and then continued.

Rahel missed Yechezqel. He had left for his apprenticeship in Jena last summer. There had been loud disagreements. Papa wanted Yechezqel to apprentice with him so that he would take over the shop, but Yechezqel rebelled, wanting to create the fancier shoes that men and women would require in bigger towns and cities. Their four older brothers had already left to marry and have families of their own. The oldest brother became a carpenter, while the three other brothers became scholars and teachers. Except for Yechezqel, all were far from home. The brothers didn't want to apprentice with Papa—he wasn't an easy man.

Rahel came to another path. It wasn't as overgrown as the first one she had passed. Her feet took her to a grove of trees and stopped in the shade of her favorite tree. Looking up at the highest branch, she slipped off her shoes, letting her toes dig into the ground. The basket joined her shoes. She closed her eyes and inhaled, smiling, listening to the breeze gently rustling the leaves.

* * *

"Both feet solid? Left hand on the next branch?"

Rahel looked down at Yechezqel. "Yes."

"Don't look down! Look where you're going to reach next!"

One branch higher than the other. This was fun! Why weren't girls allowed to do this? She was so excited when her brother agreed to teach her. Left hand, right foot. Reach. Pull the weight up. Stop. Breathe. Look to the next branch. Left hand firmly grasped on the next branch. She looked around, wanting to reach the sky, wanting to pull a cloud down and hold it. Oh! An empty bird's nest.

She was disappointed that the next branch was too thin to hold her. "I can't go higher!" There was more whine in the statement than she wanted.

She carefully made her way down. Once her feet touched the ground, she smiled. "I want to do this by myself!" She made a little hop for emphasis.

"Do you think you can? You won't need me?"

"Yes! Yes, yes!" She put on her shoes and untucked her skirts from their temporary britches fashion, fluffing them out so they would fall over her legs correctly.

* * *

Rahel reached into the basket for one of the apples. Her days were long and dull since Yechezqel left for his apprenticeship. She turned and left the little grove. At least she could sneak to her tree when Mama was called away and Papa was distracted with cobbling in his shop. The last time she had climbed was the previous summer.

* * *

Shoes by the tree trunk and her skirts in makeshift britches, she ascended until she was high enough to look around. She moved to a lower branch which looked sturdy enough to sit upon. Legs dangling, she enjoyed this moment—until Mama came into the grove. Her mother was foraging for plants that would become salves and teas. Rahel became very still, swallowing her breath, trying to control her rapid heart, and hoping her mother wouldn't see her shoes. She scooted a little closer to the trunk, thinking it would be better concealment. Unfortunately, in doing so, her foot brushed loose a twig and leaves. At the same moment her mother picked up one of Rahel's shoes, the leaves landed on her head. She brushed them off, looking up.

Mama gasped. Her eyes wide with an expression that was equal parts anger and mortification. *"Ja, was machst dort oben?!* Come down!" With very little choice, Rahel slowly climbed down. The intake of air from her mother's gasp was enough suction to pull her from the branches.

"Untuck your skirts! Put these on!" Her mother was too impatient to wait for Rahel to come for her shoes. She threw them at her. "What if someone, a man, saw you?! What if the rabbi saw you?!"

Rahel untucked her skirts, at the same time shoving her feet into her shoes. Not waiting for her to stand fully upright, her mother grabbed her left ear; she caught at her mother's arm, trying to pull away. "Mama! Ow! No one saw me! No one!"

"I won't have it!" Her mother shook her for emphasis.

* * *

She took the path on the left at the fork. The path to the right would lead her to the town. She took another bite of apple. She recalled the aftermath of that tree-climbing incident.

* * *

Rahel's mother bade her stay outside, so she sat on the ground by the door, absentmindedly twirling a leaf by the stem between hera thumb and forefinger. Even though her left ear still slightly stung and was ringing, she listened to her mother roaring at her father. The thud-thud, thud-thud-thudding told Rahel that Mama was stomping back and forth in front of Papa. His daughter was almost to her womanhood, and she was behaving as if she were a boy! A ruffian boy at that! Rahel was terrified what punishment would be meted out.

"She needs more chores to occupy her days. Perhaps the *rabbanit* would speak with her," Papa offered.

Rahel stopped twirling the twig and twisted around to look at the door as if she would be able to hear better.

"More chores?! Involve the *rabbanit*?!" There was silence. Silence that lasted too long, Rahel thought.

"We will not involve the rabbi's wife! She'll follow me in everything I do when she's not doing her chores. That's tThe only way that I can keep watch over her at all times. She'll learn how to make teas, salves, and poultices. She'll come with me to my visits. In time, she'll learn to be a midwife."

"Our rabbi won't allow her to learn to be a midwife until she's fully a woman and married. Unthinkable."

"Speak with the rabbi on this matter. Ask for special dispensation. Tell the rabbi that she'll begin with learning and visiting. She'll only join me when she's in her womanhood."

There was another silence, then a creak of wood from Papa's chair. "I will." Rahel could imagine Papa's expression and the feeble nod he used when he was reluctant. Rahel's oldest brother called it "resignation" and told her what it meant.

* * *

She heard rapid footfalls behind her and turned. She quickly moved off the road, out of the way of a woman she had never seen before. The woman was wild-eyed, wearing a dirty apron—*blood, maybe*—and holding her skirts high so that she wouldn't trip over the hem. As soon as the madwoman was out of sight, Rahel resumed her journey.

Rahel finished the apple and tossed the core to the side of the road just a few paces away from Sarah and Netanel's home. She stood on the stone that was the threshold. She hesitated to knock when she heard howling from the other side of the door. It was an animal sound. She had seen goats and sheep give birth. Could it be any worse? She gave a single, courteous knock and then opened the door. Mama and Beryl were by Sarah, who was in a makeshift bed. The woman was drenched in sweat, her face contorted in the worst kind of agony that Rahel had ever seen. There was another howl. Mama was calmly encouraging Sarah. It was the stench of blood co-mingled with sweat that caused Rahel's stomach to roil. She dropped the basket where she stood and clapped a hand over her mouth when there was that awful tingling in her jaw. She ran out the door, not bothering to close it behind her. She bent over for the eaten apple to splatter on the ground. A moment later the remains of the morning meal joined the apple. Bits of it landed on the toes of her shoes and the hem of her skirt. She straightened and wiped her mouth with the back of her hand just as she heard a tiny cry.

"A boy! Netanel's prayers have been heard! A blessing to your house!" Mama said.

Rahel walked back in with the intent to wash her mouth with water. Instead, she witnessed the after effects of birth and ran outside for a new wave of retching. It was lucky for her shoes and dress there was really nothing left to splatter. She didn't know how long she stood there clutching her stomach while she willed her vision to clear.

Rahel felt a hand on her left shoulder and turned around. Her mother looked past her at the splatter on the ground and then back at Rahel. "It happens sometimes. But you'll get used to it."

"Getting sick or helping through childbirth?"

"The latter. I hope the rabbi is agreeable to allowing you to assist."

Rahel hoped he wouldn't.

MAIL FROM UP-TIME

By George Grant

Mail From Up-Time

George Grant

Grantville Post Office

May 1635

"S hit!"

Bernita Jenkins' day had *started* normally. The work had even been rather light. She and Selma had sorted the flats and letters, thrown parcels, sorted and distributed the accountables, and gotten a start on putting up the box mail before the window was due to be opened. Once the initial rush at the window was past, they had finished everything else way ahead of time. Since it was Selma's morning to run the window, Bernita had time to perform one of the tasks they never seemed to get to. So she had decided to organize the storage room. Which was where she was now.

While she stood staring at the tray of years-old mail she had just found and grumbling under her breath, the stirred-up dust got to her, and she started coughing. She needed to do something with the mail anyway, so it seemed like time to leave the storage room.

She was still riffling through the letters with one hand while carrying the tray on the other forearm when she got to the postmaster's office. Pam Sizemore was sitting at her desk doing paperwork. Normally, Bernita would expect her to welcome an interruption while she was at such a boring task. And she probably would this time too, until she found out why Bernita had come to see her. "Pam?"

Pam looked up. "Yes, Bernita?"

"Remember the day after the Ring of Fire?"

"How could I forget it?" Her eyes went to the tray Bernita was holding. A perplexed expression crossed her face, then cleared. "Uh-oh. Is that what I think it is?"

"Yeah. All that mail we didn't know what to do with. We set out a tray for everybody to put it into, expecting to figure out what to do with it later. Only, apparently, later never came. I just found it in the storage room."

"Damn. Well, nothing for it now but to go through the mail and figure out what to do with it all." Pam paused. "Since you found it, I assume you're far enough ahead of today's work to be doing something discretionary in nature?"

"Yeah. I was organizing the storage room. I guess that's not what I'm going to be doing for the rest of the day."

"You guessed right. We're the Dead Letter Office now. Go through it and do what you can to figure out who gets what, and...divvy up the rest to pass on to whoever you think should look at it to see what they can figure out."

The Next Day

Gunther Mackenstein pushed the hamper full of mail out through the swinging loading bay doors and over to his mail truck. He was not happy with some of today's mail. Those up-timers who were working at the post office when the Ring of Fire occurred had screwed up royally and misplaced a bunch of that day's mail. Now it was up to the carriers—most of whom were down-timers, and therefore bore no blame for it—to deliver mail to customers who were bound to be unhappy. And Gunther knew who always gets blamed when there's bad news. Whoever delivers it.

He unlocked the truck doors and started loading. At least, as a city carrier, he got to drive an LLV to deliver the mail. With the gasoline restrictions, the rural carriers had had to go back to the horse-and-buggy days for mail delivery. But since the city routes were mostly park-and-walk, they could make a tank of gas last for weeks. So they got what gas they needed. It wouldn't have been secure to park a buggy and leave most of the mail in it while walking a loop.

And the LLVs would probably keep on running until somebody started manufacturing new mail trucks. After all, the oldest one in Grantville was less than ten years old at the Ring of Fire, and LLV stood for Long-Lived Vehicle. So with proper maintenance, they should last another twenty years at least.

Gunther finished loading, locked his LLV up, and pushed the empty cart back inside. After doing the necessary last-minute tasks, he walked back out and drove off to begin his route.

Over the course of the morning, Gunther didn't see anybody at any of the addresses where he delivered the old mail. But partway through the afternoon, he parked in Saint Mary's parking lot and began a loop there. He was about halfway through the loop when Stephanie Acton-Kynloche came out onto her porch to take the mail directly from him. "Good afternoon, Gunther. How are you doing today?"

"I'm well, Frau Acton. Umm...but there's mail here that was sent to your family in 2000. Since your house was outside the Ring of Fire, the Post Office, um, thought the whole family was left up-time so it never got delivered. Here." He handed her all the mail for both the High Street house and her old address, including an old parcel, and braced himself for her displeasure.

Stephanie looked somewhat downcast. She took the handful of mail and looked down at the wide, flat parcel. After a moment her face lit up like the man she loved had just proposed to her. "Oh, Gunther, thank you, thank you!" She gave him a tight hug and turned and ran inside

Gunther shrugged and walked back out to the sidewalk to continue his deliveries.

* * *

When Stephanie got inside she tossed the rest of the mail on the table and eagerly tore open the Munson's package that was addressed to her mother. She pulled off the lid and didn't even pause to think about which one she wanted to try first, but simply grabbed a piece and stuffed the first real chocolate she'd had in years into her mouth. As she was vigorously chewing, it occurred to her that she really needed to savor these, but the urge was too strong right now. She would take the time to savor the next one.

Stephanie had been working at the shoe store and living with her mother and stepfather just outside the Ring of Fire until that April second. But she had been in town at the moment it happened. One brother and two grandparents had also come through the Ring of Fire, but she missed her mother, sister, and other brother fiercely. Since the Ring of Fire had made her homeless, she had moved into the High Street house with her eighty-seven-year-old grandmother, who really should have had somebody living with her already. Then Grandma died later that same year. The house had still belonged to Grandpa, but he lived at Prichard, so Stephanie had been alone.

By the time Grandpa died in 1634, Malcolm had proposed to her and she'd accepted. They were now married and in the process of trying to buy the house from Grandpa's estate, using her share of the inheritance as their down payment. In the meantime, they were renting it from the estate.

Stephanie set aside the National Geographic magazine and the catalogs, popped another chocolate into her mouth, and picked up the top letter and a knife and slit the envelope. It was a bill. About five years overdue. From a country several centuries in the future.

An hour later

Malcolm Kynloche finished taking care of his horse and tack and left the former garage. Entering the house through the kitchen door, his first impression was that a storm had come through. The table was littered with paper, and there were even a couple of small, dark brown papers on the floor. Open on the table was a wide, flat box with a grid of empty holes, each perhaps an inch across.

And Stephanie was sitting in the midst of it, hair disarrayed, crying.

He pulled a chair up close, sat in it, and put an arm around her. "Why, Lassie, whatever is the matter?"

"Oh, it's...you see...I mean..." She gulped and sniffed. "They found some old mail at the post office. Mail that," she hiccupped, "should have been delivered to my old home, the day after the Ring of Fire. Most of it's nothing much, but this...this one..." She sobbed again and held out an unopened envelope.

Malcolm took it and looked at it. It was addressed to Stephanie Acton. The return address was someone named Benjamin Short, of Middlebourne, West Virginia. The name almost sounded familiar, but who it was wouldn't come to him. Stephanie seemed to think he should recognize the name though, so he said as little as possible. "Aye?"

"You see it, don't you? I haven't seen him since 2000, and I was pretty sure he...he..." She sobbed again. "I know I'm just being silly. I love you, and I've married you, and we're going to have a baby, so it shouldn't matter. But I can't help it. This brings it all back, and I don't regret a thing, but I can't help my emotions. Don't you see?"

"Don't I see what?"

"I thought he was going to propose to me! And I missed him so badly for so long after the Ring of Fire. What if he was proposing in this letter?"

"In a letter? Is that how up-timer men propose to their women? I dinna recall hearing that afore."

Stephanie turned her head and looked directly at him for the first time since he had come home. "Oh. You're right. That probably isn't it." She tried to stifle a sob. "But what if it is? It could be, you know. It would just make me feel so bad."

He held the envelope out to her. "Only one way to find out. Open it. Then at least you'll be feeling the proper feelings for what he had to say, and after they've run their course, you'll be able to put them away. There is nae sense in dragging it out this way."

She nodded sharply and took it from him. "I guess you're right." She picked up the knife and slit the envelope in one quick motion. Took the letter out and started reading. And after half a minute gasped and started laughing so hilariously, and with such fits and starts and gulps and gasps, Malcolm couldn't tell whether it really was laughter or just another form of crying. She held the letter out to him.

He took it from her and started reading. After half a minute he set it back down on the table and squeezed her tight. "So, it would seem he was breaking up with you, instead. Still, I canna tell from the way you are whether it makes you happy or sad."

Stephanie was still so much in the throes of the emotions surging through her that she had trouble forming her words. "I...don't know...either. Both...at once, I guess. And guilty...and relieved...and angry..."

"Well, whatever you're feeling, I'm here for you."

That seemed to calm her some, so she was mostly just sniffling. "You know what the worst part is?"

"Nay, what is it?"

"I ate every chocolate and barely remember them."

The Small Crisis
George Grant

Under a tree at the Blackshire Elementary School playground

ground

October 1631

"Get it off! Get it off!"

"Stop struggling!"

Jack pushed Hans' hands closer together and removed the Chinese finger trap from his forefingers.

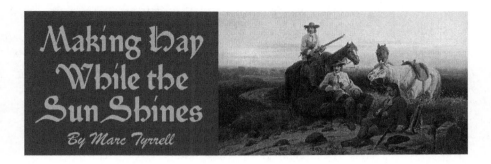

Making Hay While The Sun Shines

Marc Tyrrell

Refugee Center near the Power Plant

Wednesday, July 2, 1631, 7:35 a.m.

Hermann Peter Stieff looked up as his name was called. *"Hier!"* He stood up and took the bag he was handed, even as the man who handed it to him called out another name. Sitting back down, he opened the bag and slowly pulled out its contents.

"What is it, Sergeant?"

"My clothes, *dummkopf*." Shirt, pants, vest, jacket, socks, shoes, belt. Standing up, he pulled on his pants and threaded the belt through them, feeling it carefully. *They missed the coins!* He quickly pulled on his shirt, put the vest on over it, followed by his jacket, socks, and shoes in quick order. He glanced around, and most of his men had bags as well.

"Get dressed," he growled. "It looks like the Americans were serious about hiring us." His men hurried to obey.

Stieff looked into the bag and saw that there was more. *My satchel! Oh, thank the Good Lord!* He carefully pulled it out and checked inside. *Paper, quills, ink, writing board, books, spy glass. What's this?* He felt around and pulled out a purse, which he opened, noting the silver inside. *I don't believe it!*

The bag now appeared empty, but he checked it again, anyway, finding a single piece of paper with printing on it. *Roman script? And very strange German.*

Present this voucher to any American soldier once your disposition has been decided. Number 487. The message was printed, but the number was handwritten.

Stieff glanced up at his men, who were hurriedly dressing. "Check your bags carefully. See if there is a piece of paper similar to this"—he held up the note—"inside." He watched his men empty their bags and, one by one, hold up similar pieces of paper. He nodded. "Make certain you keep that paper."

"What is it, Sergeant?"

"I'm not sure, Töpfer. What I suspect it is, however, is a receipt for our weapons." Stieff produced a rather cold smile, one his men knew well. "Did any of you notice how few Americans there were at Badenburg?" Seeing their nods, he continued. "Well, they won because of their guns, and I suspect they don't have enough people to use them all." He could see interested looks on his men's faces. "They need people—trained soldiers—but they probably don't need our weapons." He shrugged. "At least not for any real battles."

"Now that's an interesting observation—*Sergeant,* was it?" a voice spoke from behind Stieff.

Stieff whirled around and saw one of the Scots cavalrymen who was working with the Americans. "Yes, Sergeant Hermann Peter Stieff. And you are?"

The Scotsman smiled. "David Munro. I'm here to take you and your men, at least those who agreed to join the New United States Army, to your new lodgings and show you around the town. Those of you who are not joining up should follow me to the exit station and then check in with the Red Cross." He gave a quick wave. "Gather your belongings and follow me." Munro turned around and walked toward the doorway.

Stieff looked around and nodded. "Let's go." He turned to follow Munro. Once through the door, they found themselves under a large awning with tables forming a channel.

Munro waved them to the first table. "Do you all have your vouchers? That piece of paper your sergeant was waving around?" When he saw the nods, he smiled. "Good. Hand them in to the nice man here, and you will be given your weapons back. He gave a short laugh. "No pikes, but everything else. If you need pikes, they will be issued to you. You will have to sign for them, and you will also be issued your enlistment bonus in the local currency."

Stieff cocked his head. "You're giving us silver as well?"

Munro shook his head with a rather odd smile. "The Americans don't use silver. They use a paper currency. I still don't know what it is backed by, but all of the merchants in town take it with no question, while they generally won't take silver. If you have silver and need to convert it into the local money, you can do so at the bank." Munro gave a slight snort. "My cousin, Hamish, thinks they're all daft but"—he shrugged—"it seems to work for them. Sergeant?" He waved towards the table where another Scot was sitting.

That man called in English, "Number 487. Ah repeat, number 487."

Stieff passed the Scotsman his paper.

He asked in German "Are you enlisting?"

"No."

Switching to English, the Scotsman added, "Did ya get that, Davy?"

"Aye, ah did. Most of his men are enlisting."

"Gud." Turning back to Stieff, he switched to German. "Shouldn't take long for your weapons to get here."

Stieff nodded. His weapons clattered as they hit the table. "One sword, one dirk, two wheellock pistols, one rifle. Powder and shot." The Scot behind the table looked up at him. "Is that everything you had, Sergeant?"

"Yes."

"Then sign here."

Stieff nodded and signed, collected his weapons and moved aside.

"That's quite the gun you have there, Sergeant." Munro's eyebrows were raised.

Stieff shrugged, but a smile played on his lips. "Made in Augsburg. I can hit a man at three hundred yards with it, but it takes forever to reload."

"And why, pray tell, would an infantry sergeant be needing a gun like that?"

"My men are scouts." Seeing Munro's still raised eyebrows, he elaborated. "Oh, you cavalry do most of the scouting, but you're not quiet about it, and you don't do well in forests or rough terrain. That's what we would do, at least,"—here Stieff's face clouded—"when we had a commander who could find his ass with both hands. Our last one?" He shrugged and shook his head.

Munro nodded with a wry grin. "Ah, yes. The value of scouting seems to be dependent on the intelligence of the commander. Too many of them are enamored of the romances or of their own 'brilliance,'"—there was a sarcastic tone to that—"for them to realize that reality is what it is, and not what they believe it to be."

Stieff snorted. "Isn't that the truth!" Stieff glanced at the table, and saw that Töpfer had his weapons and Kleinst was now waiting. Only the two of them were joining Stieff in trying civilian life. Glancing back at Munro, he asked, "So, what do my men have ahead of them?"

Munro shrugged. "I'm honestly not sure. The Americans say that they will be given 'basic training' as well as orientation, whatever they might be." Munro shrugged. "From what little I have heard, they will be training most of your men to use up-time shotguns."

"And what are they?"

"Did you see people with short guns that fired multiple times shooting what looked like grapeshot? Where each shot could hit multiple targets?"

Stieff frowned for a moment, then nodded. "I think so. They don't seem to have much range, though."

It was Munro's turn to nod. "Aye, that's true. Then again, most soldiers can barely hit the broad side of a barn at fifty paces, so why worry about range?"

Stieff laughed. "Well, my men can, and I think it would be a waste of their skills to retrain them on these 'shotguns.' Maybe they can get rifles instead?"

Munro shrugged. "No idea, but it's worth asking. What other skills do your men have that set them apart?"

"The usual for scouts: some drawing, counting large groups, estimating distances, tracking." Stieff shrugged. "We all speak Italian, German, Flemish, and Spanish. Most of us speak at least one other language; I've got Latin and English myself. That's about it."

Munro was nodding. It wasn't uncommon for mercenaries to know multiple languages. He shifted to English. "Ye say ye can speak English? How well de ye ken it?"

Stieff smiled and replied in the same language. "Somewhat." He glanced upwards quickly. "I have not it used much these three year gone."

Munro switched back to German, smiling. "Then you should have no trouble in Grantville." He pointed at a table that held several women. "That's the Red Cross over there. You should talk to them about lodgings and jobs." Munro held out his hand. "Good luck to you, Stieff."

Tip's Bar, Deborah
Saturday, July 5, 1631, 4:05 p.m.

"Hamish, lad, it's glad I am to see you!" David Munro waved at Hamish. "Sit yerself down and have a drink." David glanced over at the bar, pointed to his beer glass, and waved two fingers. The bartender nodded and started drawing two beers.

"Davy, y'er lookin' well, cousin!" He was interrupted by the arrival of their beer. "Ah, thank ye, lass!" Hamish took a long sip, then smiled. "That's good, Davy. It's no tha' American horse piss. Nah, where was I? Och, aye, tell me all about the battle at Badenburg."

David leaned back and shook his head. "'Twas nary a battle, Hamish. They attacked and got trounced; broke in five minutes." He took a long pull at his beer. "Then we went in and the Americans brought in their braw trucks, and it was all over but the shouting. Did ye hear 'bout the lass what hid her sister and bairns i' the crapper?"

"Aye." Hamish shook his head and pondered his beer. "Ah hear she got married to one o' the Americans this past day."

David nodded. "That she did. And spent the last few days choosin' 'mongst the prisoners who c'd stay and who be an outlaw." He drained his beer and waved for two more. Hamish swiftly drained his as well. "Well, and now Jackson has doubled his men. And what o' you, Hamish? How is life wi' young Riddell in yer wee unit?"

Hamish's mouth stretched into a smile. "Oh, 'tis a surprise ev'ry day, Davy! Why just last week, we brought in a short company o' horse and a half company o' foot. Jackson was a mite put out about it, but young Mackay hired the horse, and Jackson picked up three in four of the infantry."

David turned to smile at the barmaid who placed their beers on the table and took away the empties. "So that's where von Thieren came from?" He nodded in approval. "A braw man, for all he's an officer! His men look good, and his camp followers are a wonder." He snorted, "Best I've ever seen, to tell God's honest truth."

Hamish was nodding. "Aye, that they are. And now, young Riddell tells me, he's goin' to be gettin' reports coming in from all over. I dinna ken how it happened, but he seems to have made some friends who are willing to share what they know wi' him." Hamish took a long pull on his beer. "We're goin' ta be workin' a lot from now on, and no' gettin' out much. I'll tell ya true, Davy, I'm no looking forward ta that!"

David was nodding while he took a sip of his beer. "Ah may be able ta help wi' that, Hamish." At Hamish's raised eyebrow, he continued. "Sev'ral of the men we captured at Badenburg were trained as scouts; infantry, but scouts f'r all that. Eight of the men decided to enlist wi' Jackson, but I'm thinkin' that they could be a braw addition to yer wee unit."

Hamish sipped his beer, while leaning back and thinking. "Tha' might be good, Davy. See what else ye can find out about them and I'll talk wi' young

Riddell. Mind, we dinna have the space for them now, but we should by th' end o' next week."

Slate Lane House, Grantville
8:45 p.m.

Paul Riddell leaned back, stretching his neck, and heard several vertebrae snap. It had been a long, but very productive, day spent mostly talking with Gagnrad. A week ago, Gagnrad's nephew, Martin Zöllner, the innkeeper at the Black Tree Inn in Nauendorf, had offered to send information to Paul. Today, Paul and Gagnrad had gone over that offer and clarified what types of information would be most useful. By the end of the discussion, Paul realized that Martin was merely his point of contact into a larger network.

Gagnrad had spent most of the day teaching Paul one of the coding systems the network used. It was a fascinating mixture of substitution cipher, anagrams, and poetry/song forms. The messages, at least the ones Gagnrad had Paul decipher, appeared to be just chatty letters. Paul had to write the system down since it was too complex for him to remember. Gagnrad had frowned, then sighed, only telling Paul to keep it secret. He had left shortly after dinner, saying that he would return in ten days or so.

Paul heard the front door open and glanced out of the office to see Hamish walk in unsteadily. *He's been drinking again.* Paul sighed and called out "Hamish! A word?"

Hamish nodded and made his way carefully into the study, sitting down in front of the desk. "Ah, Paul. Just the man I'm wantin' to see. Ah may have found us some people who can help wi' the workload."

Paul cocked his head, trying to judge just how much beer Hamish had taken on. "Where? In the bottom of a beer barrel?"

Hamish glared at him. "It's no' ma fault! Ah've been drinkin' tha' horse piss you Americans call 'beer,' and now ah've found some of the real stuff, an' it's hittin' me a wee bit." Hamish's glare softened. "Na, where was I? Ah, yes. I've found us some people. Well, me cousin Davy has. Seems tha' some o' the folks from Badenburg are scouts." Hamish leaned forward. "Infantry, but scouts for all that. And"—Hamish leaned back and waved expansively—"if we ever want to get out again, we're gonna be needin' some folks as can do the work here."

Paul leaned back and thought about what Hamish had said. He found himself nodding. *Scouts should, at least, have the right mindset for intelligence work, even if they'd need training.*

Roth House
Monday, July 7, 1631, 1:57 p.m.

Balthazar Abrabanel leaned back and thought about what Paul Riddell was telling him. *For an amateur, he is producing decent intelligence, at least at the tactical level.* Paul's short descriptions of the villages north of Grantville towards Erfurt and further up into the Harz Mountains were detailed, as was his enumeration of Tilly's units in the area.

Paul had moved on to a new topic. "Just last week, I managed to make contact with some people who will be sending me similar information on an ongoing basis. Much of it will be coming in the form of chatty letters, but some will be coded. I don't know how large an area these people cover, or how detailed, or timely, the information will be yet. I do, however, trust the people in this network."

Balthazar cocked his head. "Why do you trust them, Paul?"

As Balthazar listened to Paul's answer, he could tell that Paul was concealing something. "One of the people in this network has interests that are aligned with ours. He believes that what we stand for will benefit his people."

Balthazar was tapping his teeth with his forefingers as he thought about Paul's answer. *He's hiding something, but do I push him on it?* "Paul, I think we will need to double-check whatever they send you." Paul started to look mulish. *Interesting! I think he DOES trust them!* Balthazar waved a hand. "They may well be sending us what they believe is good information, but we have no way of knowing how accurate or precise they may be. We don't know what their limitations are and, before we act on it, we need to know those limitations."

He could see Paul thinking that through. Finally, Paul started to nod. "All right, I can see that. But,"—Paul leaned forward—"if we're going to be double-checking them, we are going to need more people. Hamish, Martin, and I just can't do all of it!"

Balthazar was nodding. "True. Who else do you want? I doubt we can get any more up-timers, so you'll have to recruit from somewhere else."

Paul was nodding. "Hamish tells me that there are some people captured at Badenburg who may be suitable. I've made arrangements to keep track of them."

A field outside Heilsberg
Wednesday, July 16, 1631, 7:30 a.m.

Stieff, Töpfer, and Kleinst had been hired as guards for a haying crew right after picking up their weapons. This was the second haying trip Stieff had been on, and the third village their group had helped so far on this trip, and he was quite enjoying the experience of being welcomed by villagers, for a change. Stieff scanned the fields, checking for any potential problems.

"See anything, Sergeant?"

"Not a thing, Töpfer, not a thing." Stieff smiled. "I have to say, this has been a pleasant change from soldiering."

Töpfer snorted. "We still have a fair few soldiers with us." He pointed towards a cluster of twenty pikemen, six cavalrymen, and five shotgun-armed infantry. "Quieter, though, and I have to say that we are eating better."

Stieff nodded. "I'll give the lieutenant points for organization. Anyway, we're really only here to protect the up-timer and his marvelous machine."

Töpfer smiled. "I've never seen anything like it. Imagine, ten acres harvested in just three hours! We'll be finished haying here tomorrow, if this keeps up."

"From your lips to God's ears, Töpfer!" Stieff hadn't stopped scanning the horizon while he had been talking, and now something caught his attention. "Hold on." He reached into his satchel and pulled out his spyglass. Opening it up, he scanned the horizon slowly, then quickly closed it. "*Scheiße*! Töpfer, take over scanning, I need to talk with the lieutenant." Stieff took off at a ground-eating lope towards the cavalrymen.

"Lieutenant Autenheymer!" he called out as he approached.

"Yes?"

"There's a column of smoke coming up from around Teischel. It could be raiders from one of Tilly's units."

Autenheymer nodded, and turned to two of the cavalrymen near him. "Horst, Ernst, go check it out—quickly. Scout and report back." Turning back to Stieff, he asked, "What would be your recommendation if it is, *Herr* Stieff?"

"I doubt it is a feint to draw our guards away. There's really no other way for anyone to get a force here except for the way we came." Stieff frowned. "If memory serves, any raiders hitting Teischel can only go two ways from there: towards Milbitz and us, or towards Teischroda and down towards Rudolstadt."

Stieff shrugged. "If it's a small band, I think they would avoid Rudolstadt and come this way, so I would recommend that we hide *Herr* Hawker's machine, leave the non-combatants behind, and move towards Milbitz. We can probably defeat a small band. If it is a large band, then I would suggest you send several riders to carry a warning to Rudolstadt."

Autenheymer smiled. "Very good, *Herr* Stieff. I believe that you were a sergeant in your previous company?" At Stieff's nod, he continued, "Very well, Sergeant. I want you to take command of both your men and of our shotgun-armed troops. Talk with Sergeant Halvorson, who is commanding the pikes and work out your tactics. We will move towards Milbitz in five minutes." With that, Autenheymer wheeled his horse and rode off to talk with Preston Hawker. Stieff turned and went to talk with Halvorson.

Stieff had seldom talked with Sergeant Ulric Halvorson, and only on business. Halvorson was not the type of man who invited familiarity. Unlike Stieff, he was in the NUS Army. "Sergeant Halvorson."

"Yes, Stieff?"

"We have a situation." Stieff explained while Halvorson listened.

Finally, Halvorson nodded and turned towards the shotgun-armed infantry. "Pieter! You and your men are under Sergeant Stieff's command. Obey him as you would me." Turning back to Stieff, he said, "Let's go."

Stieff nodded. "Pieter, bring your men with me. We are moving towards Milbitz." He looked around and spotted Kleinst, giving him a "come hither" signal.

"What's up, Sergeant?"

"We're moving towards Milbitz. Possible raiders in Teischel. Get Töpfer. Weapons, powder and shot, minimal food. Go."

"Right." Kleinst moved off in Töpfer's direction, while Stieff gathered the shotgun troops together.

"We'll travel light—weapons, ammunition, enough food for one meal. Milbitz is not far away, just under a mile. Go and get what you need." Stieff watched them break apart and run to their tents. Soon he was joined by Kleinst and Töpfer. "Boys, looks like we will see some action today after all. We're off to Milbitz in about five minutes."

Pieter and the rest of his men came back quickly. Within four minutes of his sending them off, they had all returned and were moving out. Halvorson already had his pikes in a column marching towards Milbitz. As Stieff led his men out, the up-timer, Preston Hawker, moved towards him carrying his rifle. "I hear you're in command of the guns, Hermann."

Unlike Halvorson, Hawker *was* gregarious. He and Stieff had talked many times. Stieff had even been over to his house for dinner and met his family. Often, they talked about Stieff's rifle, which seemed to fascinate Hawker. In turn, Stieff had fallen in love with Hawker's 30-06, a BAR 1918A2, semi-automatic monstrosity that Hawker called 'Betsy.' "I am, Preston. But what are you doing here? You should be with your machine."

Preston snorted. "Fat lot of good I'd do there by myself, buddy! Nope, I'm going with you, Hermann."

Stieff gave a theatrical sigh, which just caused Preston to laugh. "Nice try, Hermann. Ain't gonna work, though." Preston's face grew serious. "'Sides that, you may need what I've got," he said, slapping Betsy's stock. "I brought four hundred rounds with me in twenty-round magazines. I figure if I buy it, you can use my gun until it runs dry."

Stieff just shook his head. "Preston, stop being...What was that term Carolyn used? Oh, yes, such a 'drama queen'! This could just be a false alarm."

Preston shrugged. "If it is, we've lost a couple of hours. If it isn't, then maybe we can do some good."

Outside Milbitz
Twenty-five minutes later

Stieff looked through his spyglass towards Teischel and frowned. That's a LOT more than a small band of raiders! There must be eighty or ninety of them—mainly infantry, thank God!

Lieutenant Autenheymer called out, "Stieff! Halvorson!"

Both trotted towards him.

Autenheymer looked worried. "According to Ernst and Horst, there are around a hundred men attacking. To the best of my knowledge, the count had only fifteen men stationed there, plus the militia. It appears to be mainly infantry, and the count's men are holding them so far. Suggestions?"

Ulric's face was stony. "We can hit them on the flank and try to force them back."

"Stieff?"

"Agreed. They're stuck into the village right now. If Sergeant Halvorson takes the pikes and the militia we have,"—that was twenty men with guns, many over fifty years old—"that should relieve the pressure on the Count's men. If I take my men and the shotgunners, we should be able to smash them hard enough that they will be disorganized. That's when you can rout them with your cavalry."

Autenheymer nodded. "Fine, let's do it. Stieff, send the militia to Halvorson. I believe your men have rifles?" At Stieff's nod, he continued. "I'll want you to target officers, sergeants, and chosen men in that order, and do it from as far away as possible. Kill the head, and the body dies."

Stieff felt his eyes growing rounder. That is NOT a normal order from an officer! "Yes, sir."

"Good." Autenheymer had a small smile on his face. "Ulric, hold back until Stieff has sown some confusion. Then I want you to advance slowly—menace them, but don't charge. Have the militia fire on them, for what good it will do. Try to make them gather against you and hold them in place. Can you do that?"

"Sure, Johan...Sorry, Leutnant Autenheymer. What then?"

Autenheymer smiled coldly. "Then we send Hermann here forward with the shotguns, while I hit them in the rear. I want those arschlecker attacking Stieff, and then I want them dead. Understand?"

"Not a problem," Ulric said with an equally cold smile.

Stieff, however, had a question. "Where did they come from, Lieutenant, and are there more coming? I've no problems with killing them, but I think we need to save some to interrogate."

Autenheymer thought for a moment, then nodded. "Good point, Stieff. We'll do that. Try to wound a sergeant."

On the outskirts of Teischel
Twenty minutes later

Stieff led his men, including the not-to-be-dissuaded Preston Hawker, up a field on the west side of Teischel, separated from the village by a small stream. Halvorson and Lieutenant Autenheymer had crossed the stream and were moving north. He could see the raiders moving slowly south through the village. "Right. We stop here and shoot at them. Rifles first, shotguns when I say so. And shotguns, lie down. I don't want them seeing you. The rest of you, take a knee—smaller target that way."

"Hermann, you're a better shot than I am. Use mine, and I'll use yours." Preston held out Betsy.

"Are you sure, Preston?"

Hawking nodded. "Yup." He slipped a bag off his shoulder. "Here's the extra magazines."

Stieff and Hawking traded guns and ammunition. Bringing Betsy up to his eye, Stieff looked through the scope then quickly chambered a round. *I think I'm in love.* He sent a bullet into what was obviously a sergeant, watching his right leg buckle. *Yup, love at first sight.* He scanned for another target, fixing on one who fell before he could pull the trigger. "Good shot, Preston."

"Thanks, Hermann." Preston was already ramming. "Ya know, this really is a bitch to reload!"

Stieff didn't say anything, instead letting off another shot into a man encouraging his mates. *What was that song? Oh, yeah! "Another one bites the dust!"* He started humming as he scanned for his next target, quickly shooting the bearer of a halberd. He had just got a mounted man in his sights when he saw him reel back and slump off his horse. "Good shot!"

Töpfer called out, "Thanks, Sergeant!"

"Kleinst, are you slacking?"

A rifle shot answered him, and he saw two people going down, throats blown out by the same bullet.

"Damned show off!"

Kleinst just laughed and started to reload.

Stieff pulled his eye away from the scope and tried to see the bigger picture. It looked like the raiders had stopped their movement into the village and were regrouping. "Get ready, boys. I think they will be coming at us soon." He went back to the scope and spotted a man giving orders. A second later, that man was on the ground with his brains blown out.

A mounted man flashed between the buildings before Stieff could get his sights on him. "Okay, everyone. Make sure you are reloaded, and let's let them come at us. We want them out of the village, so we want to give them an easy, inviting target. Shoot anyone you see with a gun."

Stieff and his men were about fifty yards from the small stream that marked the western boundary of Teischel. Halvorson was about a hundred yards south of Stieff's position on the eastern side of the stream, and Stieff had no idea where the lieutenant and his cavalry had gotten to. The sounds of fighting inside the village itself had diminished to an occasional shot. *Right, they're gathering. They should either attack us or retreat within the next minute.*

"Left side, muskets!" Kleinst's call was punctuated by a shot. "*Scheiße, missed!*"

Stieff tracked leftwards and saw five or six men with muskets coming around a building. Taking aim at the lead musketeer, he shot and saw him fall. "Reload, Kleinst, and don't miss next time." Another shot rang out. *Probably Preston.* A musketeer had his gun wrenched out of his hands and stumbled backwards, sending two other musketeers sprawling.

Stieff shifted his gaze back to the center buildings and saw pike-armed raider troops emerge to form a line. The raiders didn't appear to have noticed Halvorson's troops, who were now only forty yards away. *Right, make sure they are focused on us.* Stieff sent a bullet into the right-hand file leader, blowing his shoulder apart.

"Kleinst! Töpfer! Preston! Take out the musketeers!" Stieff concentrated on the pikemen, who were now a good ten feet out from the buildings in a triple line and marching towards them. He shot as quickly as he could, while maintaining aimed fire. *Click. Damn!* Stieff reached into the bag Preston had given him and grabbed another magazine, quickly exchanging it for the empty one.

As he brought his rifle back up, he heard the militia's muskets fire, and Halvorson yelled "Charge!"

Stieff yelled, "Shotgunners! Take them!"

The five prone shotgunners came to their knees and started to rapid-fire their weapons into the pikemen. Stieff shifted his aim to the musketeers and shot the last one he could see just as Halvorson's pikemen hit the disintegrating line of raiders. "Cease fire! Targets of opportunity only!"

Many in the raiders' pike line dropped their weapons and ran back into the village. A flurry of pistol shots rang out from within the village, and Stieff could see Autenheymer's cavalry chase fleeing men and cut them down. Within a minute, the fight was over, and Stieff stood.

"Halvorson! Are we clear?"

Halvorson looked around. "Yes. Get your men in here and take over prisoner duty!"

Stieff nodded and beckoned his men forward.

Stieff addressed the leader of the shotgunners. "Pieter, good work there. Take over guarding the prisoners, but make sure your guns are fully loaded."

Pieter nodded and spoke with his men while they walked towards the village.

Northern entrance to Teischel
9:15 a.m.

Stieff, Autenheymer, Halvorson, and the count's local commander, Sergeant Hans Zimmerman, gathered together to figure out what to do next. Zimmerman had a slash across his right cheek that was slowly leaking blood. "*Leutnant*, I really think you need to send a rider to the count and keep your men here until we can get reinforced."

Autenheymer was nodding. "I'd already planned on doing that, Sergeant. But if they have more people, and I have to assume they do, then we don't have enough to effectively defend Teischel."

"Let me interrogate the prisoners, sir. I should be able to find out how many more they have," Stieff said with his cold smile.

Autenheymer stared at him. "I was thinking of having Ulric do the interrogations."

Stieff's smile hardened. "Have him as my backup, sir. I have no doubt he would get information. I'm just not sure how good that information would be."

Autenheymer cocked his head. "Now you're sounding like Captain von Thieren, Stieff." He shook his head. "Fine, what do you need?"

Stieff thought about that as a softer smile played on his lips. "Beer. Maybe some *kuchen* if there's any here. If not, bread and cheese would do."

Lieutenant Autenheymer started laughing, then waved him onwards. "Have at it, Stieff. Sergeant Zimmerman, can you arrange for beer and something to eat?"

Zimmerman nodded and headed off, shaking his head, followed by Stieff.

"Ulric, act as backup for Stieff, please."

Ulric cocked his head and spoke very quietly. "Do you really think this will work, Johan? I'm pretty sure I can get the information we need."

Autenheymer smiled wryly. "I'm pretty sure you can as well, Ulric. The thing is, anyone you interrogate will probably be out of it for days, if they live."

Ulric got a sour expression on his face, but nodded.

"If Stieff can get the same information without using torture, we will be ahead. Think about it for a minute: we don't need information immediately and, honestly, the Americans have an absolute hatred of torture. I'd rather not piss them off. One other thing, Ulric."

Ulric raised an eyebrow.

"We're working with the Americans now, and how did they treat Stieff and the others they captured at Badenburg?"

"Hunh? They hired them of course. Why?"

"Think they might hire these people as well?" Autenheymer asked with a slight smile.

* * *

Stieff walked down the line of wounded men and spotted the first man he had shot. *Thirty-five or forty, decent clothes, equipment in good repair...probably a sergeant or chosen man.* He went over to him and squatted down. "How's the leg?"

The man looked up at him with a wry smile. "Feels like I've been kicked by a mule, neighbor. Is this the point when you pull out a knife and start working on me?" He had an odd accent, sort of Swiss, but not quite.

Stieff gave a short laugh. "Actually, I thought we might share a couple of beers and just chat. If that's agreeable with you."

The man barked out a laugh. "Sure, why not?"

"Hold on and I'll get them." Stieff stood up and looked around for Zimmerman, who was approaching with tankards, a flagon, and a plate of something. Going over to Zimmerman, Stieff said "Thanks, Sergeant." A quick glance at the plate showed dark rye bread, sliced cheese, and some type of pickles. Zimmerman gave a nod, then walked off, while Ulric took up a guard stance about twenty feet away.

Returning to the wounded man, Stieff squatted down again, placed the plate on the ground and poured beer into both tankards. "Here you go, comrade." He saluted with his tankard and took a sip. "Help yourself to some food if you'd like."

"Thanks." The man sipped his beer and took a piece of cheese, put it on the bread, and started to nibble. "Not that I'm not grateful or anything, but can I ask who you people are?"

Stieff took a sip and smiled. "The name's Stieff, Hermann Peter Stieff. As to who we are, well, have you heard of the Ring of Fire?"

The man's eyes widened a bit. "The priest traveling with us mentioned something he called the Pit of Hell that appeared within a ring of fire, inhabited by witches. Is that what you're talking about?"

Stieff got an extremely wry smile on his face. "Yeah, that's it. They captured me a couple of weeks back at Badenburg. No witches that I've seen, but they are...different." Stieff shrugged. "Pretty decent people from what I've seen."

"Well, not what I expected, but..." The man shrugged, then took another sip from his beer. "I'm Hans Lutz, Hermann." Taking another sip, he asked, "What are they like to work for?"

Stieff shrugged. "Better than most, Hans. After they captured us, they gave us a choice: join our army or pick up a job. Well,"—here he gave a slight laugh—"except for the *arschlöcher* who got declared outlaws and kicked out."

Hans snorted. "Always a few in every group, Hermann. The world's better off without them. So,"—Hans grabbed another piece of bread—"what happens now?"

"Depends on you, Hans. We'll probably take you back to Grantville, and you can make your choice there." Stieff glanced at Hans' leg. "Well, you'll probably need some medical care first."

Hans took a slow sip of his beer, then began nodding. "I think I believe you, Hermann. Which puts me in a bit of a quandary." He gave a quick snort, "O *strompede mi* as the song says." Hans looked at Herman carefully.

"I've got a wife and kids back at our camp. I'd really like to get them back. Any chance of that?"

Stieff just had to shrug. "Honestly? I don't know, Hans. It would have to depend on how many troops there are and where your camp is and,"—another wry grin—"we just don't have many troops here."

Hans snorted. "More than enough to blow us away, neighbor!" He shook his head, trying to clear it. "We're camped up near Neckeroda, two to three miles away. The captain sent us down here to secure Teischel. The lieutenant in charge, well, he 'expanded' on the captain's orders. I think the captain was trying to put a scare into the count of Rudolstadt. Well, doesn't really matter *why* he did it, does it?"

"Not really, Hans."

Hans nodded. "There should be about eighty or so pikes and a dozen musketeers left in the camp. Plus our camp followers." He cocked his head. "Think you can take that?"

Stieff had to think about that. "Maybe, under the right circumstances, but it's not my call. I'd have to be an idiot, or an officer, to think we could take them in a full-out frontal assault."

Hans snorted. "Why be redundant? Anyway, you sound like a sergeant, so you probably know what you're talking about. So, what are you going to do?"

"Go talk with the lieutenant in command," Stieff said with a grin. "Strangely enough, he doesn't seem to be an idiot—probably because he was a chosen man up until a couple of weeks ago." Stieff stood. "Have some more food and keep an eye on your men while I go talk with him."

Hans nodded and placed a piece of cheese on some bread, handing it to the man beside him. "Here, Müller, you probably need this."

Dieter Müller was a chosen man in charge of musketeers who had been knocked out by a grazing shot to the temple. He took the bread and cheese. "What do you think, Sergeant?"

"Wait and see, Müller, wait and see. But the pickles are good, so eat up."

* * *

Stieff, Autenheymer, Halvorson, and Zimmerman stood in a circle while Stieff told them what he had learned. At the end of the debriefing, Autenheymer nodded. "Suggestions?"

"We can take them, Jo...Lieutenant." Ulric said.

"Stieff?"

"I agree with Sergeant Halvorson, Lieutenant, but I'd feel better if we had more men, especially more cavalry."

Autenheymer nodded. "Sergeant Zimmerman?"

Zimmerman looked somewhat abashed, but spoke out. "I agree we probably could take them but, as Sergeant Stieff says, I'd feel a *lot* better if we had more men." He closed his eyes for a moment. "And I have to say that the count hasn't authorized me to do anything more than defend this village."

Autenheymer was nodding. "Most of the troops we have here actually aren't in the NUS army. They're guards for the haying we've been doing for the count. The only actual troops are our five shotgunners and Sergeant Halvorson here, along with my cavalry who are in Swedish service. So, here is what I'm going to do. First, I'm sending two of my men, one to the count and one to Schwarza asking for reinforcements. Second, I want to make certain that the prisoners are in no position to escape while we wait for those reinforcements. Comments? Suggestions?"

Stieff coughed. "Might I suggest that I and my men move towards Neckeroda and scout them out?"

Autenheymer looked at Stieff. "If you want to, Sergeant. It will be at least six hours, probably more, before any reinforcements show up. Do you need any support?"

Stieff thought about that. *Autenheymer doesn't act like a typical officer, so...maybe.* "I'd appreciate having one of your men to act as a courier, sir."

Autenheymer nodded. "Done. Get your men ready to move out. Anything else?"

"Let me talk with Lutz again, sir. His wife and children are in that camp, and I'm fairly sure he is willing to switch sides, as long as he can get them back."

"Do it." Autenheymer looked around. "All right, we have a plan. Unfortunately, most of it is to wait for reinforcements. Let's go."

* * *

"Well, Hans, we're going to try and get your wife and kids."

Lutz looked at Stieff. "Really? You don't have enough troops, Hermann."

Stieff got a slight smile on his face. "You're right, Hans. That's why we're calling for reinforcements. They should be here in five or six hours." Stieff squatted down. "Look, what can you tell me about your captain? Is he likely to stand down if he's faced with overwhelming force?"

Hans thought about that. "Probably. He's a professional, not an idiot. Why? What do you have in mind?"

"Did you see our shotguns, Hans?"

"You mean those guns that kept on firing? Oh, hell yes!" Hans shook his head. "I nearly crapped myself watching our pikes fall!"

"What do you think your captain would do if we had fifteen or twenty of them, plus another fifteen to twenty cavalry?"

Hans paled. "Damn." He closed his eyes, then opened them. "He won't believe how powerful they are until he's fighting them. He'll be slaughtered."

"Would he believe you and, maybe, a demonstration?"

"Maybe. But only with a credible threat."

Stieff nodded. "I think we can arrange that. Are you willing to talk with him?"

Hans thought about that. "Same surrender conditions as you?"

"Yes."

"All right, yes, I'll do it." Hans snorted and glanced at the hole in his leg. "Well, at least as long as I can get myself there."

Forest outside of Neckeroda
12:45 p.m.

"What do you see, Kleinst?"

Kleinst looked at Stieff. "Probably the same thing as you, Sergeant. About eighty pikes and maybe a dozen musketeers. Pretty organized camp."

Stieff nodded and patted Kleinst on the shoulder. "That's what I see as well. We'll go with that. Got your sketches?" Kleinst handed over a sketch of the camp. "Thanks, Jacob. Keep an eye on them while I get this to our courier."

Stieff headed back from the tree line and walked over to the courier Autenheymer had detailed for him. "Here you go, trooper. These are the sketches of the camp and our best guess as to troop strength."

"Thanks, Sergeant. I'll get these to Lieutenant Autenheymer." The trooper took off, leaving Stieff behind.

Teischel
3:25 p.m.

Johan Autenheymer watched as a troop of twenty cavalry led by Heinrich Bauman trotted into Teischel. "Good to see you, Sergeant. Anyone else coming?"

"We've got some infantry trying to stay in the saddle coming behind us. They should be here in another fifteen minutes or so." Bauman had a small smile on his face. "And the count's man is sending a couple of wagons, along with twenty or so men to guard the prisoners. They won't be here for another hour or so."

Autenheymer nodded. "What are the infantry armed with, Heinz?"

"Shotguns, as you requested. They're part of a new training unit, mainly captured at Badenburg, but there's also one or two who used to be under Ulric."

Autenheymer was smiling. "Excellent! This should go well for us. Settle the men in and then come over and help me look at what our scouts have."

Twenty minutes later...

Bauman was looking over the sketches of the camp and estimated numbers when Ulric Halvorson walked up. "These are impressive, Ulric. Your work?"

Ulric shook his head. "No. That's from Stieff and his men. They've been up there keeping an eye on the camp for the last few hours."

Bauman cocked his head. "Stieff? Don't think I know him."

"Captured at Badenburg. He hired on as a guard with the haying machine, along with two of his men. He's solid. He says he was a sergeant, but he thinks like an officer. Well,"—Ulric gave a small smile—"the way an officer should think."

"Is that a comment about me, Ulric?" Lieutenant Autenheymer asked with a small smile of his own.

"Not at all, Jo...Lieutenant."

Johan rolled his eyes. "Let's just leave it at 'Johan,' shall we? And I agree, he does think like a good officer. Have you told Heinz about Stieff's suggestion yet?"

"Not yet."

Johan nodded. "It's a pretty ballsy idea, Heinz, but I think it can work. The basic idea is to present an image of overwhelming force and get them to surrender without having to fight. Stieff talked with one of the sergeants we captured and he's willing to help."

Bauman was looking interested. "Why would he help?"

"Because his wife and kids are at the camp."

Bauman thought about that, then shrugged. "That may help, but I doubt his captain is going to believe we have overwhelming force. We'll have, what, twenty pikes, twenty-five cavalry, and twenty-five shotguns, but he will probably think they are hunting pieces. If he's got eighty pikes and a dozen muskets, he'll probably think the odds are closer to even."

"Probably." Johan was nodding. "Which means it's in his best interest to talk. Stieff seems to think that he can talk him into a surrender." Johan shrugged. "I don't know if he can, but I'm inclined to let him try, since if we do end up fighting, it will be a slaughter."

Forest outside of Neckeroda
4:50 p.m.

Stieff was waiting for the column just before the road left the woods, but out of sight of the camp. "Lieutenant, good to see you, sir. I see we've been reinforced."

Autenheymer nodded. "That we have, Sergeant. And I brought your new friend Sergeant Lutz along as well. Have there been any changes since your last report?"

"None, sir."

"Good. Alright, we'll give the men a short break, while we plan our deployment."

Fifteen minutes later...

The column, led by Lieutenant Autenheymer, Stieff, and Sergeant Lutz, moved along the road out of the forest. Stieff could see rapid movement in the camp and, within several minutes, pikes forming up, with musketeers on the flanks.

"Deploy," Johan called out.

His own pikes moved from column to a double line, with shotgunners on either flank. Sergeant Bauman led the cavalry over to the left flank.

Johan glanced around, making sure the men were in position about four hundred yards from the camp. Seeing that they were, he slowly walked his horse forward, flanked by Stieff and Lutz, stopping halfway to the camp. "How long do you think we should wait, Sergeant Lutz?"

Lutz, who had been watching the camp closely, finally nodded. "Shouldn't be more than a couple of minutes, Lieutenant. I'm pretty sure I can see Captain Columberg now. I think he's just waiting to get two more men mounted, which shouldn't take long."

Johan nodded. "Thank you, Sergeant." Turning to Stieff, he asked, "Are you ready for this, Sergeant Stieff?"

"I am, Sir." Stieff had an interesting look in his eye. "I think this should work, and with minimal bloodshed."

"I pray so, Hermann!" Lutz said quietly. "Captain Columberg is not an idiot. He will want to get the most information he can before he goes into a fight." The expression on Lutz's face turned sour. "Unlike that stupid puppy who was supposedly commanding us in Teischel." Lutz spat on the ground. "May he rot in Hell for what he did."

Stieff raised an eyebrow, while Johan just looked questioningly at Lutz, who sighed. "Politics, Lieutenant. Captain Columberg felt he had to hire the puppy to keep our employers happy."

Stieff snorted, while Johan just grinned. "Yes, that happens all too often, Sergeant." Johan glanced back at the camp, where he could see three riders slowly emerging. "Heads up, men. Looks like we will have company soon."

Lutz was watching closely. "Captain Columberg, Sergeant Desax, and,"—he squinted—"I'm pretty sure that's Lieutenant Flury." He glanced over at Johan. "Well, Lieutenant, looks like you've got the top people coming out."

Johan smiled. "I'm honored. I think." He waited until the riders were twenty feet away, and gave the captain a short, mounted bow. "You must be Captain Columberg, sir. I am Lieutenant Autenheymer of von Thieren's Company. Beside me, I have Sergeant Stieff and, as I am sure you already know, Sergeant Lutz from your ill-fated, earlier operation."

Columberg looked to be about forty, strongly built with short brown hair and a rugged face. He gave a nod. "Well, if Hans is here, he's probably already told you who we are, but let's do the civilized thing. I am Captain

Pieter Columberg. Beside me, I have Lieutenant Jorg Flury and Sergeant Amos Desax." His smile twisted. "Might I ask, Lieutenant, just what your intentions are?"

Johan matched his smile. "Our intentions, sir, are to secure this area and to keep it secure."

Columberg looked at him quizzically, before pointing towards Neckeroda. "As you can see, Lieutenant, Neckeroda is both secure and quiet. I had sent Lieutenant von Oberschweinestall to secure Teischel. From Hans' presence, may I assume that that did not occur?"

"May I, Lieutenant?" At Autenheymer's nod, Lutz continued. "The lieutenant lived up to his name, Captain. He decided that we had to 'conquer' Teischel, and we were stuck into the village when Lieutenant Autenheymer and his men intervened."

Columberg closed his eyes and took a deep breath before opening them again. "How many did we lose?"

"At last count, we have thirty-four captured, including wounded. The *schweineficker* cost us over fifty men. Luckily for him, he is amongst the lost."

Columberg quickly scanned Johan and Stieff's faces, finding them bland and uninformative. "Well, Hans, I suppose I should say something about you using his nickname, but I find I don't really care." His face got hard. "Far better that he is dead, otherwise, I would have to 'talk' with him." He took another deep breath, then turned back to Johan. "Lieutenant, you said your intentions were to 'secure the area'. Might I ask who you are securing it for?"

Johan was already nodding. "An excellent question, sir. We are securing it for the count of Rudolstadt and for the New United States."

Columberg frowned. "The count of Rudolstadt is no supporter of Count Tilly or the imperial cause. As for, what did you call them? The New United States? I have never heard of them."

Johan nodded. "They are, as their name implies, 'new.' Sergeant Lutz tells me that you have heard of the Ring of Fire? Well, they are the people who lived inside the Ring, transported by the will of God back through time over three hundred years." At Columberg's incredulous look, he hastened on. "I didn't believe it either, Captain. But I have been in their town and met several of them. They call themselves 'Americans,' and I have been forced to change my belief."

Columberg's face went still, then his eyes flicked towards Lutz. "Have you seen anything that would support such an outrageous claim, Hans?"

"Maybe, Captain. I saw several of their musketeers firing more than ten shots in a minute. They shredded our pikes." Lutz looked perturbed, but carried on. "Pieter, they can shoot way more rounds than *any* gun I've ever heard of. Does that mean they came from the future? Damned if I know, but it *does* mean they can turn the rest of our men into dog meat if they want, before we can even touch them with pikes."

Columberg looked concerned, then stilled his face. "All right, Lieutenant. I will provisionally accept that you have such weapons."

Stieff gave a short cough, and Autenheymer glanced at him, then gave him a nod.

"Captain," Stieff said, "rather than take Sergeant Lutz's word, which is accurate, might I suggest a small demonstration?"

"What do you have in mind, Sergeant?"

"Let me suggest, sir, that I show you exactly what one of our guns can do." At Columberg's look, he continued. "May I suggest, Captain, that you send one of your men back to your camp and let them know we will be doing a demonstration. And, if possible, could he also bring back something we could use as a target? Maybe a straw tick?"

Columberg looked at Stieff, then nodded. "A good suggestion, Sergeant Stieff." He turned and looked at his lieutenant. "Jorg, go and tell the men what's happening and grab something we can use as a target, would you?"

Flury rode back towards the camp, while Columberg turned back to Autenheymer. "And what do you hope will happen after this demonstration, Lieutenant?"

"I hope, sir, that you will seriously consider surrendering, with full honors, before we find it necessary to try each other at arms."

Columberg just stared at Autenheymer, then started shaking his head. "Well, I'll say this for you, Lieutenant; you've got great big brass balls." He snorted. "Let's see what this demonstration shows, shall we?"

Stieff spoke up. "If I might suggest, Captain, that you and I go to our line and you can pick out any trooper there with a gun."

Columberg thought about that, then started to smile. "Lead on, Sergeant." He kicked his horse into motion As they approached the NUS line, Columberg was all eyes. *They look like fowling pieces, but sleek.* Finally, they reached the line, and Columberg looked over the troops. *Damn! They are confident! No fear at all.*

"Maybe this one, Sergeant?" Columberg pointed to a trooper.

Stieff nodded. "Certainly, sir. Trooper, follow us, please." The man slung his shotgun and followed Stieff and Columberg back. By the time they reached the centerpoint, Lieutenant Flury had returned with a straw tick and was setting it up as a target.

"Well, Sergeant. This is your show. Please, go ahead."

Stieff nodded. "Trooper? Whenever you're ready. Fire at full rate, then reload and fire again."

The trooper nodded, then took a firing stance. *Clickety, Boom, Boom, Boom, Boom, Boom.* A quick reload, followed by *Boom, Boom, Boom, Boom, Boom* and silence. Columberg had turned white during the demonstration as the straw tick ceased to exist.

"Well... *Scheiße!*" Columberg looked over at Stieff. "And how many of those guns do you have, Sergeant?"

"Twenty-five here, Captain."

"I think we need to talk terms, Sergeant."

Grantville High School
Saturday, July 19, 1631, 9:45 a.m.

Balthazar Abrabanel leaned back, his fingers tapping his teeth as he watched Frank Jackson and Paul Riddell out of the corner of his eye. They had just finished debriefing Lieutenant Autenheymer, Captain Columberg, and Sergeants Halvorson, Stieff, and Lutz. "Well, that was interesting."

Jackson glanced at him, then turned to Riddell. "What I'd like to know is why we didn't know about Columberg earlier, Lieutenant."

Riddell looked over at Jackson. "Lack of manpower, General. It's as simple as that. I have three men, including me, to collect and process reports. That's not enough. I need more people, and people with the right mindset."

Before Jackson could say anything, Balthazar leaned forward. "I believe that Lieutenant Riddell is correct, General. I have been reading some of his preliminary reports from his new sources. They are fascinating, and I believe that he should try to develop stronger ties with them. Unfortunately, that means he will have to be out in the field, with a bodyguard, and that leaves just one man to collate all of the *other* sources."

Jackson closed his eyes and took a deep breath, letting it out slowly. "Fine. Who do you want, Paul?"

"I'd like Stieff and his men, General."

Jackson opened his eyes. "Stieff and the two men with him were civilian guards. They're not in the military, so if you want them, you'll have to recruit them."

A small smile played over Balthazar's lips. "I believe, General, that the other eight men under Stieff's original command *are* in the military. Maybe you could assign them to Paul?" At Jackson's nod, Balthazar continued. "Paul, try to recruit Stieff. He has the right mindset, and I found his interrogation technique fascinating." His smile shifted towards a grin. "Anyone who can use beer and pickles to make an entire unit change sides is someone we could use."

Paul wore a matching grin. "I agree." The grin disappeared as he turned to Jackson. "What can I offer him, since he's already turned down a sergeant's position with us?"

Jackson grimaced. "Offer him a commission as a lieutenant."

Paul nodded, but before he could say anything, Balthazar spoke. "An excellent suggestion, General, especially if he is placed in charge of his old team. And, of course, if he is going to be made a lieutenant, then you will want to promote Paul to captain." Balthazar leaned back and looked serious. "After all, we can't have any confusion in the chain of command, General."

Jackson was looking mulish, but then shook his head and chuckled. "Fine, Balthazar. It's your shop, so—*poof*—Paul, you're a Captain. Now go out and recruit Stieff."

Paul just shook his head with a wry grin. "Of course, General."

Tip's Bar
Saturday, July 19, 1631, 3:35 p.m.

Hermann Stieff looked around the bar and smiled. Preston had introduced him to the place a week ago, and he found its relaxed atmosphere quite charming, even if they did chill their beer. Still, on a warm July afternoon, a cold beer was a pleasant enough diversion. He took another sip while watching the crowd. *They're friendly and optimistic.* He grinned. *I think I really like this place. I know I like the attitude!*

The door opened, and someone walked in. Stieff glanced in his direction, squinting against the sunlight. *Oh, damn! It's one of the officers from this morning. I wonder what the hell he wants!* The man looked around, walked over to the bar and ordered a beer, leaning back against the bar and surveying the room until his eyes met Stieff's and he nodded. He said something to the bartender, who laughed and handed him his beer, whereupon he walked towards Stieff's table.

"Mind if I join you?"

"Help yourself. Lieutenant, was it?"

"Captain, now." He said with a smile. "But this is off the record, so you may as well call me Paul." His smile grew larger.

Stieff cocked his head, but waved him to a chair. "Well, then, you may as well call me Hermann. What can I do for you, Paul?"

Paul sat down and took a careful sip from his beer. "Sorry, still getting used to how strong this is. Tasty, though."

Stieff laughed. "Well, I tried a couple of what you call beers a few weeks ago." He shook his head. "How in the world did you Americans ever think that small beer was beer?"

Paul snorted. "Damned if I know, Hermann." He frowned for a moment. "Something to do with the First World War, I think, but I don't know any of the details." He shrugged and his face cleared. "Anyway, I wanted to talk with you about a couple of things."

Stieff got a rather sardonic grin on his face. "I expected as much, Paul. What did you want to talk about?"

Paul matched his grin with a wry one. "As of Monday morning, the men who used to be under your command are being assigned to my unit."

"Really? And what, if I might ask, is your unit? Scouts? *Jäger*?"

Paul was shaking his head. "I don't think you have the concept in this time. I'm running, well, sort of, Military Intelligence. Our main job is to track enemy units, and also figure out other things. So, I guess," Paul shrugged, "we're sort of like scouts on steroids."

"'Steroids'?"

"Sorry, up-time term. It means a magnified effect, so think of your concept of scouts, but expand it."

Stieff cocked his head. "Scouting out the entire field of a campaign, maybe?"

Paul nodded and took another sip of his beer. "Yeah, something like that. But we're also interested in people's attitudes, their health, the state of their crops, politics, and all sorts of other things."

Stieff's eyebrows furrowed. "Wait! You mean like Tacitus in the *Germania*?"

Paul's eyebrows shot up. He knew the reference, and had read the *Germania*, in translation, for one of his journalism courses. His prof had used it as an example of how publications created perceptions of reality. "Exactly, Hermann. Like Tacitus."

Stieff leaned back and sipped his beer. "Interesting. And, I suppose, necessary, since you come from so far in the future. Hmmmm." His brow furrowed again in thought. "What will you be using my men for?"

"Mainly gathering information, but some of the collating as well. Making sense of what the information means or could mean later." Stieff nodded. Paul picked up his beer and continued. "What bothers me, Hermann, is that I'm likely to get some of them killed."

Stieff stiffened at that. "What? Why!"

Paul slumped back in his chair. "It's simple, Hermann. I know how to collate information, and I can build networks, but I don't know squat about how to actually use your men to their best effect to get what we need." Paul shook his head. "I'm afraid that my ignorance will end up getting some of them killed, and I would really prefer to avoid that."

Stieff relaxed a bit, took a sip of his beer and thought about what Paul had said. *Odd that an officer would admit to ignorance, but, well, up-timer.* "I would too, Paul. Well, if I can help, just let me know."

Paul cocked his head to the side. "I was hoping you would say that, Hermann. What would you think of joining my unit? As a lieutenant, in command of your men and second in command of the entire unit? I could certainly use you."

Stieff opened his mouth, about to refuse, then slowly closed it. *Oh, hell.* He leaned back and sipped his beer while he thought out the implications. He eyed Paul carefully. *I think he's serious about this. And, he's right, he won't know how to use my men. Damn!* "Paul, that's an interesting offer. But while I've read Tacitus, I don't know how to get that type of information."

Paul leaned back, smiling. "Not a problem. I can teach you—and your men—how to get it." Leaning forward, smile gone, he continued. "Hermann, I need you. Moreover, Grantville needs you, and your men need you. I can't do this by myself."

Stieff just stared at Paul and slowly shook his head. *You are a damned manipulative bastard!* "Paul, you aren't fighting fair."

Paul smiled. "All's fair in love and war, Hermann."

"Fine, I'll join you."

Paul's smile grew larger. "Hermann, I think this is the beginning of a beautiful friendship."

Among the Faithful
Bob Finegold

"What have I done unto thee?" – Numbers 22:28

Worms, Rheinpfalz (Rhineland Palatinate)
June 1635

"**G**randfather! A *Korrespondenzausschüsse* column occupies Mainz!"

Christian burst into his grandfather's study, the horrible news of protestors being shot and summary hangings trembling on his lips. At the sight of the dour-faced men gathered within the room, however, Christian stopped short. One of the *Bekanntmachung* he clutched in his hands, notices that the old man had commanded him that morning to post throughout the city, slipped from his grasp and spiraled slowly to the Flemish carpet, settling softly as an autumn leaf upon the pastoral scene depicted in threads of burnt crimson, brown, orange, and gold.

The air in the room was leaden with the men's stares and the knife-sharp silence that followed the interruption of guarded speech. He recognized the men: Father Engel, Christian's uncle, the skeletal, thin-lipped deacon of St. Peter's, who scowled at him as if he could see Christian's every sin, real or imagined; Herr Wagner, the barge master whose muscled arms and protuberant belly strained the indigo fabric of his doublet; Herr Amstkeller, the *bürgermeister's* thin-faced master of coin, who dabbed perspiration from his brow to either side of his widow's peak with a lace-trimmed handkerchief; and Herr Schreiner the broad-shouldered master carpenter, his pockmarked cheeks flushed above his thick mustache, one tip of which he tugged in vexation.

Christian did not see his grandfather until the back of the old man's hand struck him across the cheek, the old man's signet ring cutting him, felling him to the floor. The notices he held showered about him.

"What did I tell you about entering my study without being summoned, boy?" Christian's grandfather said, his voice a threatening rumble. But when was it not?a

"I'm sorry! I'm sorry!" Christian scurried back over the forest, mountains, and grazing sheep of the carpet to avoid being kicked. His grandfather's boots were *cuir bouilli*, the hardened leather molded into elegant designs that could leave painful patterned bruises that took weeks to heal—*had* left painful bruises...

Herr Amstkeller muttered, "Bastard," but in the silence following Christian being struck and his cringing apology, the word tolled louder than the ticking clock upon the mantle. All eyes turned to the perspiring tax collector.

Grandfather's head snapped around. His gray hair, full and thick despite his seventy years, framed his face like a lion's mane, and his eyes were as fierce. He glared at Herr Amstkeller. The smaller man paled, and his eyes widened.

Shame warmed Christian's cheeks at the muttered epithet, yet what he felt most was relief that his grandfather's ire had turned upon another.

"Did you say something, Piet?" his Grandfather said through clenched teeth, the words grinding like the millstones in one of his many grist mills.

Piet blanched. "No, Ehrhart! I...I mean, *yes*, Herr Schopp! I say again, '*Von Gott!*' Mainz! The *Korrespondenzausschüsse* scum there are few. How could this happen? Fuchs and his *Omenträger* were watching them. And he has a man working in the *Freiheitsbögen* where they meet! How could they have—"

"How do you think?" Grandfather slammed his fist upon the desk and plucked from it a copy of the flyer Christian had been posting across Worms. Lips pressed tight, he shook it at the group of men.

"*The Jews!* Who else? They let those damn Jew-lovers into the city. Base betrayers! Filth! Überträger der Krankheit! *It was the Jews!* And where in the Rhineland has their pestilence sunk the deepest? Mainz! Speyer! And..." He trailed off, glaring at them.

"*Here!* In Worms!" Herr Amstkeller was eager to speak first and deflect Herr Schopps' anger from himself for saying aloud what was never to be said in the older man's hearing.

Ehrhart Schopp was a powerful man, a rich man—these being synonymous in Worms. He was no noble or patrician, but many of those relied on his support, goodwill, and patronage.

When *gemütlich* from drink, and Christian could not escape him and the accompanying beating, Grandfather often lectured Christian, "*Blut ist dicker als Wasser, and the blood of the covenant thicker than the water of the womb. Yet* money *binds men tighter than either blood or Christ.*"

And money was on display all around the room: the impeccable velvets, silks, and polished leathers that adorned Master Schopp himself; the many gems of his rings—although none were as brilliant or as hard as the old man's eyes; the red, gold, and pearl-beaded damask curtains; the ivory-inlaid brass clock ticking upon the mantle; the portraits of Dutch artists peering judgmentally from their gilded frames; the Greek marble statuettes poised atop fluted plinths; the ebony drinking cabinet crafted by the *ébénistes* of France and inlaid with mother-of-pearl; the Venetian glass chandelier gently clinking above Christian's head; and the intricately woven Flemish rug beneath it where Christian sprawled, fearing to move and also not to move.

Christian took no pleasure from the cowing of Herr Amstkeller or from how the other men now, overtly, took no notice of Christian or the blood seeping from the cut on his cheek—for Christian knew that, in truth, he *was* a "bastard." The word need never be spoken for Christian to be reminded of it every day, every moment, of his fifteen years.

Magdalena, his mother, Grandfather's youngest child, had died giving birth to him when but sixteen. Grandfather proclaimed that she'd wed his father, Viktor Hess, a righteous young man of good heritage, just before the lad went off to war carrying the banner of the man who came to be known as the Winter King, only to die valorously soon thereafter at the Battle of White Mountain.

It was well known that Grandfather had long maneuvered to join his peasant blood to that of the *adel*. However, that Herr Stroppe would permit such an occasion to occur privately instead of in a panoply of great pomp and ceremony...no. At best, this suggested an inconvenient accommodation regarding the timing of Christian's conception. At worst... Thus, in either case, few believed Grandfather's tale, despite the Hess family's attesting to its verity—before they moved to, it so happened, a much finer residence in Mecklenburg than they had in Worms.

Not a single portrait of Christian's father hung on the walls of Ehrhart Schopp's manor, yet those of his mother, Magdalena, graced every room.

Blood may be thicker than water, and money bind tighter than blood or Christ, but *rumor* was greater than them all.

Despite the proclamations and attestations, everyone knew Christian was a bastard, and many delighted in the wealthy Herr Schopp's disgrace—albeit never to his face.

But even they did not know the full truth.

"Up, boy!" Grandfather grabbed Christian's hair and yanked him to his feet. He gestured to the *Bekanntmachung* scattered across the carpet. "Pick these up! Finish posting them where everyone can read them. Now, boy, now. Quickly. Like the Devil's behind you and Christ's before you—for they are! Go!"

Christian swept up the papers and fled through the study door before his grandfather's boot could imprint his bottom. The hard leather boot struck the study door behind him instead, like a mallet pounding wood. The door slammed shut, the backdraft rustling the papers in his hands. A few struggled like moths to fly free. He clutched them tighter, and despite the June heat, his skin prickled with goosebumps at the thought of dropping one for Grandfather to later find in the hall.

Christian ran past more brooding paintings and impassive sculptures, his thoughts racing while his footsteps echoed behind him.

He'd posted grandfather's *Bekanntmachung* north to south from Martinskirche to Manuskirche and eastward to the main market square abutting the Bürgerhof. It was at the market where he'd overheard the buzz of news concerning the *Korrespondenzausschüsse* militia seizing Mainz. Mainz was only a two-day march from Worms! Faster, if one traveled by barge up the Rhine—unless Herr Wagner forestalled them—but could he?

People in Mainz shot and hanged! Could it happen here?

In the manse's tiled foyer, he swerved to avoid colliding with Frau Lehmann, Grandfather's housekeeper, who stepped through the open front door holding a freshly beaten rug folded over her pudgy arms. Her brow furrowed as Christian passed her. He slid along the iron-banded oak door and bounded out into the manse's courtyard bordering the Kämmererstraße and Johanniterhof.

Blinding sunshine and the cacophony of street noise struck him almost as hard as Grandfather's boot. Spray from the courtyard's burbling fountain wet his face as he ran past, the cool mist the most pleasant thing he'd experienced since awakening that morning. That pleasure and the idle thought came with its own cost, however. Squinting in the bright light, he leapt over one of the stone benches surrounding the courtyard's fountain, and his toe caught on the seat edge. He tumbled out onto the hard cobblestones of Kämmererstrasse. Angry shouts and curses erupted around him, and a mule snorted derisively.

Fearing his grandfather more than personal injury, Christian clasped the *Bekanntmachung* tight to his chest and, this time, not one sheet escaped him—but his brow struck the dung-smeared cobbles, and fiery pain lanced both his forearms as he slid across the stones.

Christian's head rang louder than the Dom's cathedral bells. He lay gasping on the sun-heated cobbles, inhaling, *tasting*, the foul smells of ordure while his heart pounded in syncopation with the ringing in his head. After several long moments, they eased, and the sounds of the world about him returned.

Loud, shrill laughter drowned out the rumbling of a passing cart and the chatter of the townspeople who parted around Christian as indifferently as the Rhine around the Lorelei. Cool shadows fell over him.

Lifting his head, Christian peered up through strands of blood-matted hair and winced at the sight of three older boys, Klaus and Heinrich Brecher, and Ulme Koepfler, whose company he strove to avoid as much as he did his Uncle Engel's in confessional.

Klaus's scuffed boot dug under Christian's bruised ribs and rolled him over. "Ha! It *is* the bastard." Klaus was the oldest of the three but shorter and stockier, built much like the barrels of his father the cooper.

"What's he got there?" Heinrich, Klaus's reed-thin sibling, stepped on Christian's wrist. A harelip twisted Heinrich's face into a perpetual sneer. "He's holding them tighter than he does his *schwanz*."

Ulme, with wild russet hair, laughed and said, "Let's see." He kicked Christian's other hand.

Flyers fluttered across the cobblestones, darted like moths between the legs of the people passing, to be crushed, sullied, or torn beneath boot heel, hoof, or rolling cartwheel. Christian's stomach clenched. He tasted bile. The fear of retching in front of the older boys was nothing to his fear of what his grandfather would do to him if the *Bekanntmachung* were not posted.

"*Ach du meine Güte!*" A deep and melodious voice spoke, more in disapproval than anger. "Here. Stop that now. Leave the lad alone."

Startled, Christian's three assailants stepped back, Ulme quickly declaring, "We're just playing! We didn't—" But one look at the man who'd spoken, and the three boys' expressions twisted from surprise and guilt to anger and contempt.

Christian gazed up. Nearly standing astride him stood a slightly built man of middle years or older, his back curved as if he carried a great weight upon it. He wore a long, loose-fitting coat of dark brown wool and a cloak of a similar dun color. The coat was cinched at the waist with a fringed woven belt secured with a simple iron ring. His eyes alone held color, blue speckled with gold like the Rhine in sunlight, their expression wary but unwavering. He had a small brown mole on the side of his nose, but his pale face was otherwise unremarkable save for a beard-like dark thatch. His hair was a deeper and richer brown than his coat. Curls like a sheep's fleece coiled beneath his cloth-rimmed conical beret—a telltale head covering as distinctive as the large yellow ring pinned to the left breast of his cloak.

Clenching his fists, Klaus advanced. "You want us to 'play' with you instead, Jew?"

Heinrich spat upon the Jew. Ulme sneered and slipped a small knife from his pocket.

Christian's own rage was equally visceral. If not for being half-beaten and bleeding, he would have cursed and struck out at the Jew as well—and yet...something was familiar about the Jew. His sudden flush of heat and anger ebbed, replaced by a queer puzzlement that slithered in his stomach like a dyspeptic eel. The Jew did not move from above him.

As the boys approached, the soft-spoken Jew straightened like a brown bear rising on its hind legs. He was not so slight as his posture and humble demeanor had conveyed. In fact, he was tall. Klaus's head barely reached the level of the Jew's chest, and the loose-fitting coat gathered more tightly about him, conforming to the muscles of a thirty-something man in his prime. His blue eyes blazed in the sunlight like one of the biblical prophets. "You *gontses*! Go!" he said, leaning toward them, his own fists clenched.

At the Jew's sudden transformation, the three boys' eyes widened, and then they turned and fled.

Like a fading gust of wind, the Jew shrank back into a meek, huddled form. Lips pressed together, he smiled at Christian and held out a hand to help him rise.

Christian scuttled back, his palms scored by the grit atop the cobbles. "Don't touch me!" Confusion churned within him. His heart raced—for he knew what others did not.

Grandfather, in the stupor of his drunks, had revealed to Christian in alternating bouts of weeping and shouting that his *Schätzchen*, his

Mäuschen, his beloved Magdalena had died in childbirth of *"a Jewish disease."*

And Christian *hated* Jews for this. All Jews. Grandfather was right. They were a pestilence.

Still seated, he picked up a *stück* of mule dung, still warm and steaming, and threw it at the Jew. "Get away from me!"

The malodorous clod struck the man's cloak and clung below the yellow rota like a second badge of shame before falling back to the cobbles, leaving a wet stain on the garment.

The Jew was still a moment, then he shrank even further, shoulders hunching, and his face sagged into an expression of remorse. He lowered his proffered hand, then bent and began to pick up the scattered flyers.

"Stop that!" Heat flushed Christian's cheeks. Rising to one knee, he snatched Grandfather's *Bekanntmachung* from the Jew's fingers.

"Is everything in *ordnung* here?" With a rattle of chain upon his gorget, a soldier garbed in the silver key on red shield livery of the *Bürgerhof* stopped before them. He glanced at Christian, kneeling on the cobbles with three soiled notices pressed to his chest, and then glared at the Jew.

Words of accusation against the Jew quivered on Christian's lips...

But they were lies, and Christian found he could not speak them.

Instead, he said, "No, sir. I fell."

The soldier frowned. "Then, *gehen sie weg!* Both of you. You're disturbing citizens."

The Jew bowed low, first to the soldier and then to Christian. He stepped aside and disappeared amid the ceaseless flow of people and carts. The soldier watched him through lidded eyes, harrumphed, and then continued onward as well.

Christian gathered up the few of Grandfather's dispersed flyers that were still legible and added them to those he'd held onto. He drew the back of his hand across his aching forehead and winced. The hand came away bloody, and he took care not to get blood on the papers. Then a thought came to him. He scattered droplets of his blood over the *Bekanntmachung*. What better way to gain peoples' attention when they passed by them? He lifted one sheet and nodded with satisfaction.

In large, bold letters splattered with blood, the top line warned:

Sie kommen für dich!

They are coming for you!

The second:

Juden! Hexen! Zukünftige Volk!

Jews! Witches! Future People!

In smaller print below was a list of their infamies and evils, those well-known as well as new perfidies, like the plague that had sickened and killed many to the west in Lorraine the winter before and that Christ alone had kept from the faithful of the Rhineland.

Now Christ called upon his children to *save* the Rhineland, called them to gather that evening at the Pfauenpforte. *Now* was the time for true believers to fight for their faith and their families; *Now* was the time for the Rhineland to fight against the too-long coddled evils of the Jews, devil-worshipers, and the licentious and heretical sorcerers of Grantville and their minions.

The last line, again in bold, was the strident cry of the Holy Crusaders:

Deus Vult!

God Wills it!

* * *

Torches crackled and tainted the air with the stench of burning pitch. Their flames rippled at the caress of the wind, rising to its touch like a child whose hair was ruffled by an affectionate hand. Cascades of sparks spiraled up into the night.

Fire loved to burn.

On a wooden platform erected before the tower of the Peacock Gate, Christian's grandfather leaned over the sea of faces like the figurehead of a sailing ship. Behind him, aligned like officers on deck, stood his son Deacon Engel and the other men Christian had stumbled in upon that morning. Their eyes glowed like embers in the torchlight, and a crimson glow surrounded them, reflected from the red sandstone walls of the Peacock Tower.

Grandfather's clenched fist rose. Its shadow loomed upon the city wall. He shook his fist at the silent crowd below him. "By now, you've heard the news from Mainz. Of these misguided who call themselves *Korrespondenzausschüsse*, our brothers in Christ who have betrayed Him as despicably as any Jew, who have taken up arms and *murdered* Christ's devoted followers, even his shepherds on Earth! '*We are* all *equal under God*,' they proclaim."

He halted and glared at the throng gathered below the platform. Murmurs and mutters rustled.

"Jews the equal of good Christians?" Grandfather's voice was iron. "Was the serpent equal to Adam? No! Never!"

From the back of the crowd, someone echoed, "Never!"

Grandfather nodded. "Are those who rebuffed Christ and salvation *equal* to those who acknowledge Christ as Lord?"

A few voices answered. "Never!"

"Never!" Grandfather said. "And each day, *more* of these betrayers of Christ crowd our streets, scurrying away from the war to the east like curs, instead of joining to help repel the Turkish invaders. Instead, they dirty our doorways, sully our markets with their cheap, gaudy wares, huddle in our alleys with their stinks and their brats, spreading disease—and conspiring. Conspiring as they did in Mainz! Will we permit them to do it here?"

"*No!*" came scattered cries, but these still few.

To Christian, most of the townsfolk appeared uncertain, perplexed, drawn out to the Pfauenpforte not by fear but by curiosity, seeking spectacle. Some had brought their children, and these paid Grandfather and his words little attention, chasing each other within the forest of adults, occasionally being caught up in a parent's arms when they drew too close.

The old man frowned at them. Christian well knew that look of ire and frustration. Memories of old bruises tightened upon his skin, but before his grandfather could castigate the crowd, a hand touched the old lion's shoulder. Christian's uncle, the Reverend Deacon Engel, met Grandfather's eyes. The deacon's lips moved silently. Grandfather's face lost none of its severity, but he stepped back, his drawn lips curving into the tiniest of smiles, his expression conveying a fierce pride in his son, the deacon—a look that caused Christian's chest to ache with longing.

Striding to the platform's edge, the reverend deacon looked upon the crowd, his gaze as unwavering as a falcon's upon its prey. The crowd stilled. Deacon Engel stood silently for an additional dozen heartbeats. The only noise was the torch flames snapping like scarlet pennons in the wind.

In a thunderous voice, Deacon Engel called out, *"'Woe unto you, scribes and Pharisees, hypocrites!'* Ye Jews! *'For ye shut up the kingdom of heaven against men.'"*

The wind shifted. Smoke swirled and stung Christian's eyes and filled his mouth with ash. He coughed and blinked away tears. Grandfather heard him from where he stood behind the deacon, his son. His gaze pinned Christian where he stood. Christian felt sweat seep from his skin.

"'Ye devour widows' houses; therefore, ye shall receive the greater damnation!'"

Around Christian, people began to mutter and shift their feet. Their faces grew animated.

"'Ye are the children of them which killed the prophets!'"

Christian knew the words, had heard them at home and at church, and yet when his own ire rose while his uncle enumerated the many sins of the Jews, he recalled the face of the Jew who, just a few hours before, had stood over him, had *protected* him from Klaus, Heinrich, and Ulme. Christian's contempt and anger ebbed and became confused. Somehow, impossibly, he'd recognized the Jew, knew him. But from where? Christian shook his head. It was not possible. He gritted his teeth and focused his attention on his uncle's words.

"'Ye serpents, ye generation of vipers, how can ye escape the damnation of hell?'"

Yes. *Vipers!* Damned vipers! All of them! All of...

The Jew's eyes. Blue flecked with gold like sunlight sparkling upon the Rhine... The small mole on the side of his nose like a wary fly...

"'Wherefore—'" The wind gusted. It wailed and blew swirls of smoke into Deacon Engel's face. He choked and then coughed vigorously. *"'Wherefore—'"* He coughed again, as loud as the report of rifles. He covered his face with the sleeve of his black cassock until the smoke cleared. When he lowered his arm, his eyes were bloodshot and his face taut, incensed by the affront of the wind as much as by those whom Christ and Church condemned. He shouted, *"'Ye are the children of them which killed the pr-prophets!'"*

Christian blinked at the repetition. The Book of Matthew had been a reading primer for him. His grandfather and uncle had insisted. Atop the platform, his uncle spluttered as he collected himself. Saliva flew from his lips like a horse brought short by its bridle—

—And Christian gasped as memory overcame him.

* * *

He'd been small, five years of age, perhaps, maybe younger, playing beside the fountain in the manor's courtyard with a ball of scuffed red leather that Frau Lehmann had given him, when the ball bounced off a stone bench and rolled out into the Kämmererstraße.

He'd chased after it.

Shouts, yells, and a shrill whinny erupted around him, but he had eyes only for his ball. Picking it up, sawdust trickling from its frayed seams, he lifted his head and saw the long brown flank of a horse at least sixteen hands tall—*adult* hands, and the scowling armored soldier who towered astride him. The animal was so close to Christian, he could feel its heat and smell its sweat, a scent like grass, earth, dust, and leather.

The horse snorted, its lips close enough to nip his ear, its bulging eyes reflecting Christian's startled reflection. Warm breath puffed against Christian's cheeks, and the horse stamped its front hooves, striking sparks from the cobblestones as it sidled sideways.

The tall soldier cursed and pulled on the animal's reins—but the man paid no heed to Christian. Leaning over his saddle, the soldier continued to strike a cloaked young man kneeling upon the cobbles with his bloodied hands raised to protect his head. The young man made no attempt to flee while the soldier continued to shout curses, his bludgeon rising and falling with loud *thwacks* upon the crouching man's hands, arms, and shoulders. With a final grunt, the soldier kicked the man in the ribs, toppling him to the grimy cobbles of the Kämmererstraße, spat upon him, and then rode away.

Slowly, without even a groan, the beaten, bleeding man rose to his knees and looked at Christian—a small boy holding his ball in two small hands. Worry creased the man's brow, but seeing Christian unharmed, the creases faded. He exhaled and then smiled. His eyes were strikingly blue and flecked with gold, and, astride his nose like a resting fly, rose a small brown mole. It twitched upward when he smiled. A large yellow ring was emblazoned on the man's cloak.

While only five, Christian knew what that meant.

This was not a man. *A Jew!*

Christian backed away and ran, again eliciting shouts of surprise and annoyance from all around him....

* * *

Christian blinked as acrid torch smoke again stung his eyes. With effort, he raised his hand to clear them. The townspeople crowded close, jostling him. Frenetic energy seethed through them. They swayed like storm-whipped waves upon the sea, their expressions angry and exultant. Christian looked about him. The crowd had grown. The entire *platz* before the Peacock Gate was alight. Rippling torches outnumbered the stars, the heavens partially veiled by smoke and scudding clouds tinged crimson by torchlight, whipped eastward by the wind.

"'...the synagogue of Satan, which say they are Jews, and are not, but do lie; behold, I will make them to come and worship before thy feet!'"

Cries answered, drowning out Deacon Engel.

"Betrayers of Christ!"

"Devil worshippers!"

Many raised fists. Among them, fists that held clubs, others hammers, and a few, to Christian's surprise, knives or old swords.

The crowd squeezed Christian. Droplets of sweat showered him from shaking heads. Spittle struck his cheek. He attempted to raise a hand to wipe it away, but his arms were pinned by the sea of flesh pressing against him. He struggled to breathe.

Father Engel shouted to be heard over the crowd. *"...Upon you may come all the righteous blood shed upon the earth, from the blood of righteous Abel unto the blood of Zacharias son of Barachias, whom ye slew between the temple and the altar!'"*

And the crowd roared.

Hate and anger swirled among them, leaping from one person to the next, from haberdasher to *hausfrau*, from tanner to toymaker, from man to woman to wild-eyed child, spiraling thick and dark and foul like the pitch smoke rising from their blazing torches.

"Plague bringers!" shouted a toothless old man to Christian's right. A matronly woman to his left screeched, *"Child killers!"*

Their shouts pierced Christian's ears, wormed their way into his own thoughts, his own fears, his own hatreds—and clawed up the inextirpable images branded there: the sneering faces of Klaus, Heinrich, Ulme, and all the others who whispered behind hands or, brazenly, called him *"Bastard!"* to his face; his mother's portrait, blonde-haired and angelic, smiling down on him from above his bed, lost to him forever by giving him life; his grandfather slouched in his padded armchair, half-cursing half-crying, his words liquor-slurred: *"She died of a Jewish disease, boy!"*

A Jewish disease.

And Christian found himself shouting with the crowd, not knowing the words he said, passion oscillating from hatred and rage to shame and guilt and then back again, ever-circling, ever-growing, stronger, wilder, as if fueled by all the pain and fear and doubt he'd held inside himself all of his life.

"'Behold, your house is left unto you desolate!'"

Did he shout that or Uncle Engel? Christian did not know. He marched beside Grandfather, the old man's leonine face crowned in fiery light and glory, the crowd yelling incoherently behind them. Down the Martinsgasse they paraded, past the uneven bell towers and latticed roundel of Sankt Martinskirche, the window a scarlet eye following them as the torch-carrying mob passed. The Stadmauer loomed to his left. The city wall resounded with the echoes of raucous shouts, off-key songs, and discordant laughter. The wall curved, shepherding them eastward, and they followed. The Martinsgasse narrowed as it approached the Jew's Quarter. The cobblestones beneath Christian's feet became pitted as if by pox, and the buildings lining the street crowded each other as if shouldering for space where they did not belong. Chipped facades and overhanging eaves cast shadows of frightful shape, but these skittered upward into the night, cast out by the bright torchlight and songs of the faithful. The chasm of the Martingasse thrummed with the cacophony of their voices, drowning out the slap of boots upon cobblestones and all other noise, making speech unintelligible yet magnificently strident.

Christian's thoughts whirled. *How marvelous it was. Glorious! The Lord's host marching, assailing the devil in his lair, exacting holy vengeance for Christ, Christendom, and*—and for Christian's mother.

Abruptly, the street opened onto the plaza before Martin's Gate. On its farther side crouched the recessed gate to the Judengasse, the "Jews' Alley," with its back against the city's wall. Spilling into the plaza around Christian, the townsfolk's cries and raucous songs dispersed into the open space, chasing the shadows up into the night, then quieted, and stilled.

The Judengasse gate was not closed or barred, the Jews not cowering behind it or fleeing deeper into its crowded burrows. Instead, a group of twenty men stood in two lines before the open gate—and not merely men, but an organized company. Each wore a black beret from which a yellow feather protruded on the left hand side. A red band, four fingers in width, encircled their right arms. They held odd-looking muskets with what appeared to be large, perforated barrels, the stocks held to their shoulders and the muzzles pointed, unthreateningly, toward the pitted cobblestones, but the implied threat was inescapable. They were unlike any group of soldiers Christian had seen, and their expressions were like stone.

Behind them, a slightly larger group of bearded Jewish men stood in uneasy formation. In an odd mirroring of the townsfolk entering the plaza behind Christian, many held household items or work implements: a farrier's hammer or a butcher's cleaver here, a tanner's knife or barrel stave there.

And partly hidden within the shadow of the Jews' gate, Christian saw the Jew who'd driven off the boys who'd attacked Christian that very afternoon and who had, long ago, suffered a beating to save Christian from being trampled by a soldier's horse. The Jew's eyes darted over the townsfolk, fear within them. They widened when they alighted upon Christian.

"*Korrespondenzausschüsse.*" Christian's grandfather growled and then spat.

Christian shivered. At the sight of the Jew and, now, Grandfather's naming the company of soldiers, Christian felt shaken from a dream. Despite the heat of the sparking torches around him, flapping like pennants in the shrieking wind, his skin prickled.

The Korrespondenzausschüsse? *How could they have come so quickly from Mainz? Is this another contingent? Are there more?* He gazed about the plaza, but it was otherwise empty. A swirl of dust hissed across the cobbles separating the mob of townsfolk from the group of militiamen and Jews. The wind eased but did not cease.

The *Korrespondenzausschüsse* soldiers numbered twenty men. However, the townsfolk still spilling forth from the Martingasse flowed out to nearly fill the plaza and numbered five times that and more.

Christian's grandfather assessed the crowd arrayed behind and to either side of him and smirked. Doubt appeared on the faces of a few, but most still trembled with zeal, psalms strident upon their lips. One cried, "*Deus vult!*" and those with swords, poleaxes, *eberspeere*, and a few, Christian noted, with muskets wormed their way through the crowd to stand beside Grandfather and Deacon Engel.

Grandfather nodded, and Deacon Engel took a single step forward. He glared at the small group of militiamen before the Jews' Gate. Silence settled save for the ceaseless hushing of the wind. One of Grandfather's *Bekanntmachung* skittered across the plaza like a spider, scratching the cobbles before disappearing out the Martinspforte.

Into the silence, Uncle Engel's sonorous voice rang out. "You whoresons and Judases! Repent! Seek Christ's mercy and forgiveness! *'Every tongue shall swear Him allegiance and none other!'*"

The crowd stirred and murmured. A few called imprecations at the column of men, but Uncle Engel's voice rose above them all. *"'Woe unto that man by whom the Son of Man is betrayed!'"*

The crowd took up the verse, growing louder with each repetition.

Grandfather strode forward to stand beside his son, the deacon. He shouted, *"Liars and hypocrites!"* in his commanding voice, one that had made his mill workers jump—and patricians and sycophantic noblemen as well. "Stand aside or face the wrath of the Lord and His faithful!"

Throughout the exhortations by Christian's uncle and grandfather and the growing clamor of the townsfolk, the *Korrespondenzausschüsse* soldiers had neither moved nor had their stern expressions changed. One, with two golden feathers in his beret, seemed to be in command. He raised his hand, his palm forward.

The front line of militiamen fell to one knee, elevated their muskets, and sighted along the strange barrels toward the crowd. The men behind them remained standing, raising and sighting their own weapons as well.

To Christian, the raised hand seemed like a halting gesture, a warning to the crowd—but it was not.

The soldier lowered his hand.

Christian saw flashes of light, smelled the acrid stench of burnt black powder in his nostrils, and heard peels of deafening thunder, detonations that silenced the exhortations of his grandfather and uncle, the high-pitched screams of the crowd, and all other sound.

Then he heard and saw nothing at all.

* * *

The tolling of the bells of Saint Peter dredged Christian up from darkness, each successive peal a hammer blow. *"Funera plango, fulgura frango*...I knoll for burials; I break the power of the lightning—"

...Seven...Eight...Nine

The bells stopped.

Nine. Christian struggled and partly opened his crusted eyes. Blurry daylight seared them, and pain lanced his skull. He swiftly closed them again. Nine in the morning, the bells had tolled, calling the faithful to Mass. The last peals faded, but a rhythmic clangor continued, mixed with the rough voices of men yelling over the clamor. Incongruously, he also heard children's laughter.

Sitting up, he caught himself on the worn frame of a pallet bed to keep from falling. His head felt three times its normal size and threatened to fall to either shoulder. He touched his scalp—and gritted his teeth at the flare of pain that resulted. His fingers came away wet. He studied them until they came into focus. Their tips were bloody. Gingerly, he touched the cloth bandage wrapped around his skull and left ear...he could not feel the bulge of an ear beneath the bandage, only sticky dampness where blood had seeped through the cloth.

Opening his eyes a little wider, he saw he was in a tiny room, empty except for the creaking pallet with its soiled straw mattress smelling of mold and urine and a chipped ceramic chamber pot that smelled like it had not been emptied in a week. The walls were gray stone, damp with dew, and blackened in places. An iron-banded door with a closed iron grille at head height filled the wall to his left. To his right, close to the mold-spotted ceiling, a small, barred window let in the beam of gray daylight with the noise from outside that had awakened him.

He was alone save for a soft squeak from under the pallet bed—merely a mouse, he prayed—and whatever vermin infested the mattress. The cell was chill. Christian shivered and shuffled to the window on shaking legs. Grasping the window ledge, he balanced on quivering toes and peered between bars of rusting iron.

The sun glowed dully behind the gray haze of morning sky, but its touch warmed his face. The air streaming through the window was tepid and damp with summer's fevered breath. Best of all, the air smelled fresh, a balm to the acrid stench of sweat, blood, and urine that permeated the cell. The fog clouding his mind and vision lifted. He looked down into the courtyard below.

A scaffold was being raised.

Ropes like coiled snakes rested on its platform. A man tossed the end of one up to another man who straddled the cross beam of the gallows and secured it in place. The man below tugged on the rope, stretching it taut, then nodded when it did not come loose. He bent and raised the end of one of the remaining coils of rope.

Christian awakened fully. His eyes snapped open wide, but he then squinted again in pain as daylight flooded them.

They're going to hang me!

Fingers still clutching the window ledge, he lowered himself and rested his cheek against the cool stone of the cell wall.

He was only fifteen! He hadn't hurt anyone!

A voice inside his head said, *You didn't have the opportunity to.*

I wouldn't have!

Wouldn't you?

The thought chilled him more than the stone. He recalled his anger, his hatred, the righteousness of his wrath, the *rightness* of meting out justice too long deferred. For Grandfather. For his mother. For the small boy trapped in an old house with a bitter old man.

Wouldn't you?

The truth? He was not sure.

What would he not do to win his grandfather's approval? To win a smile and not a scowl? A slap upon his back instead of across his face?

Christian swallowed and rose on his toes to peer out the window again.

The carpenters continued to build the gallows. Guild Master Altergott directed them as perfunctorily as he would the construction of a patrician's stable or an alewife's *bier haus*. He stopped and chatted briefly with a *Korrespondenzausschüsse* militiaman, then laughed at a shared witticism before stepping aside to yell at an apprentice who'd dropped a cradle of tools.

Herr Altergott had eaten at his grandfather's table. Christian had sat beside his daughter Melusine in Church.

Along the margins of the courtyard, children played with hoops or chased one another. A juggler practiced in a corner near a nearly completed viewing stand for the town leaders. Vendors shuffled about, setting up their stalls, anticipating a hungry crowd—a crowd who, like the town dignitaries, would come whether they wished to or not. Christian had heard in whispers that the *Korrespondenzausschüsse* required this wherever they installed their new code of law and justice—justice that was swift, hard, and public.

His stomach tightened. He slid down the cell wall and sat upon the foul-smelling floor, his back pressed against the chill stone. He trembled and tried to stifle a sob—but failed.

A rattle outside his cell caused him to stiffen. The heavy door thudded as weight fell against it.

Christian clambered to his feet, his palms pressed to the damp wall.

When a key clattered in the lock, Christian's breath caught in his throat. A small trickle of urine dripped down his leg.

Now? No! It's too soon!

With a complaining groan, the cell door opened, but the figure then revealed was not the gaoler or militiaman Christian expected, but the Jew with the mole on the side of his nose and the gold-speckled blue eyes that looked more fearful than Christian felt. A small red ribbon of the *Korrespondenzausschüsse* had replaced the stigmata of the yellow rota upon his brown cloak. The Jew's stance was tense, and his skin pale, but his face flushed with color, and his stiff bearing lessened a bit upon seeing Christian staring back at him.

The Jew murmured to someone beside him in the hall whom Christian could not see except for a dirty hand that snatched the drawstring pouch that the Jew placed within it and then withdrew. The sound of scurrying footsteps followed, echoed, and faded. The mouse under the pallet squeaked.

Christian tried to swallow, but his throat was dry. He managed a hoarse, "What are—?" but the Jew waved him silent.

Placing a finger to his lips, the Jew entered the cell and knelt before Christian, checking his injured head and surveying him for any other hurt. "Shh," he said. "Come quickly. Do not speak."

He helped Christian to the cell door, supporting him when Christian's legs trembled and threatened to give way.

The prison hall was colder than the cell and smelled fouler. Other doors lined the walls, and Christian heard faint moaning from them. In the center of the hall, a long-handled, two-wheeled cart rested on its legs. The cart's bed was covered by a foul-smelling tarpaulin. It was only when the Jew folded the tarp aside that Christian realized the smell was not coming from the tarpaulin but from the dead bodies under it. Two were adult men; one was Ulme.

The Jew lifted the boy's lifeless body and placed it atop the two dead men. "Quickly," he whispered. "Get in and lie down."

Christian struggled not to retch. He attempted to step away, but the Jew's bony fingers grasped his arm like a vise.

"Please. It's the cart or the noose."

Christian swallowed, imagining the rope pulled tight around his neck, its harsh strands abrading his skin. Shaking, he permitted the Jew to help him into the cart and arrange him like one of the corpses. But when the Jew placed Ulme's limp body atop him, the dead boy's clammy cheek pressing against his own, Christian gasped and tried to sit up.

The Jew's warm, firm hand pressed him down. "Shh, *sheifale*. Lie still. Don't speak. Don't move, or it's the gallows for us both." He placed a rag near Christian's nose. It smelled faintly of lavender. Then the tarpaulin covered the cart, and Christian was shrouded in a tenebrous dark, the bodies beside him reduced to shadows save for Ulme's glassy emerald eye staring vacantly into his own. Christian closed his eyes and shuddered.

He heard a clink of porcelain tapping the wooden slats on the opposite side of the cart and then the sound of fluid being poured. The smell was foul, of urine and shite. Christian suppressed a gag. Even with his eyes squeezed tight, they watered. He pressed his face into the perfumed rag, and the stench eased. A moment later, the Jew grunted, and the cart jerked as it was lifted and began to roll on squeaking wheels. The sound was thunderous in the narrow confines of the hall.

The cart turned right, left, then right again. Suddenly, the gloom lessened, and the wheels quieted, becoming less shrill as they entered a more open space.

"*Oi, there!*" a voice bellowed. "Halt! What have you—?"

"Dead to be buried," Christian heard the Jew call out. The cart slowed and stopped. "Prisoners who did not survive the night."

A shadow loomed over the cart. Christian shut his eyes, not squeezing them tight despite the tear-raising stench. He lay very still. The foul smell of piss and shite made it easy to hold his breath. The tarpaulin rustled as it was pulled back. Daylight warmed Christian's brow, and a waft of clean air circled about him.

"*Herrgottsackramentkruzifix!*" a gruff voice swore. The tarpaulin quickly covered the cart again, and its stench flowed over Christian like a fetid miasma. The brief respite made the noxious smell seem even fouler, cloying, constricting about him much as the zeal of the crowd had the night before. *Why did the Jew suffer it, pushing the cart with its dead and its stinks? For him?* The guard's shadow retreated. "Go! *Ach! Schnell!*"

The cart creaked as it was lifted and then rattled over cobblestones. Christian heard the muffled tintinnabulation of hammering, the basso of men's voices, and the sopranos of children's laughter, but with a thump of the cart over raised flagstones, these faded. Christian then heard people conversing as they approached and their exclamations and curses if they passed too near. Further on, the drumming of the cartwheels upon the cobbles joined a greater cacophony of crowd noise, the syncopated clopping of horses' hooves, and the shuddering rumble of other wains and wagons at what Christian assumed was a city gate when its shadow rolled over him. The soldiers here were even less inclined to check the Jew's cart than the one who'd stopped them at the prison. In a short time, the sounds of the city lessened, and the wheels of the cart settled into a tolerable grumble as the cart rolled over the dried earth of a road.

It grew hot under the tarpaulin. Sweat trickled down Christian's cheek and pooled against Ulme's chill one. With a shudder, the cart left the road and trembled over rough earth. Ulme's body shifted. His cheek slid from Christian's until they were face to face, noses overlapping. Vacant eyes, fixed in startlement, stared into Christian's. Chill, moist lips brushed his. Christian stifled the urge to vomit and turned his head.

Ulme's lips pressed against his ear.

What language did the dead speak? Do they still hate? Do they still rage? Christian shuddered and focused on the sounds coming from outside the cart.

He heard birdsong, the Jew's labored breathing, and, faintly, the ceaseless hushing and lap-lapping of fast-moving water. The cart stopped, and the tarpaulin was pulled away.

The sun shone strong and hot upon Christian's face. The Jew lifted Ulme from atop Christian and placed him with unexpected gentleness upon the bodies of the two dead men, then he helped Christian from the cart and led him to a small hummock of grass a few feet away and upwind. He and the Jew stood at the edge of a field beyond a cemetery, the unsanctified ground where executed criminals were interred. Stepping back to the cart, the Jew gathered Ulme into his arms and carried him to a long ditch, newly dug, as evident by the mounds of dark, moist earth beside it. He lowered Ulme into it as gently as if placing a babe into a cradle. The Jew crooned softly, but the words were unintelligible to Christian. Whether they were a prayer or a lullaby, Christian could not tell, but the alienness of them made his skin prickle. And yet...the sorrow and compassion in the Jew's voice required no translation. The Jew turned and interred the remaining dead bodies piled like tumbled cordwood in his cart, lifting each in turn, shepherding them to their final rest in the unmarked mass grave. He carried the stoutest adult corpse as easily as he had Ulme, demonstrating a strength that belied the cowering submissiveness he had displayed in town.

Christian looked away, not wishing to see the faces of the dead. People he possibly knew. He closed his eyes, but he could not close his ears to the Jew's sad yet consolatory chanting. Standing upon the hummock, he inhaled the scents of tended grass and flowers. In a short time, Christian sensed the Jew standing beside him. He opened his eyes. The sun was bright in the now cloudless sky, nearing noon. Beyond the Jew's cart, grave markers rose in rows. Bees hummed, alighting from one graveside flower to another.

But here, at the cemetery's edge, there were no grave markers. Just weeds, grass, the fetid ditch, and dark mounds of recently moved earth. *He was to have been buried here!* He uttered a choked gasp and then felt the Jew rest a hand upon his arm, but Christian pulled free and stumbled away from him, his foul cart, and the mass grave.

Under the heat of the sun, he again began to sweat. His stomach clenched and unclenched, nausea warring with a burgeoning sense of relief at his escape. His head throbbed with pain but even more with questions. He turned to the Jew who stood silently watching him.

"Who *are* you? Why are you helping me?" His voice sounded as squeaky and shrill as the Jew's cart.

The Jew wet his lips, opened his mouth, then closed it. His shoulders sagged. "I am Rabbi Yifta Yosef Yaspha ben David. I...I was a friend of your mother."

Christian gaped at him. "My mother? Friends with a Jew?"

"Does that sound so impossible?"

Christian didn't answer.

A skylark warbled and sped over their heads. A second skylark chased it, answering. The rabbi watched them, looked down at his hands, clasped them, and began speaking.

"I met your mother when I was a boy, a year before I was called to the Torah as a Bar Mitzvah—my coming of age. She was three years my elder. I saw her swimming in the Rhine, singing to herself, and thought her a siren. Then her song became cries, and she thrashed in the water. My fear that she would drown was greater than my fear that she was one of the *lilin* and would drown me. I jumped in and pulled her to shore, where we caught our breath among the lavender, her favorite scent.

"In my wet clothes, I must have looked like a drowned puppy, but she, in but her shift, was a perfect pagan goddess, if one rubbing out the cramp in her bare calf." Rabbi Yaspha smiled. "Magda—" The rabbi stopped and cleared his throat. "The truth?" he asked Christian.

Christian could only nod.

The rabbi took a breath and said, "Your mother, *Fräulein* Schopp, was scandalously uninhibited, mischievous, sly in avoiding her chores, and quick to laugh. She was insatiably curious—and unreservedly kind. *'Eshet chayil mi...*A woman of valor who can find? For her price is far above rubies.'"

The memory seemed to weary the rabbi, and lifting his cloak, he sat down. Plucking a blade of grass, he twirled it slowly between his fingers. "Your mother and I became secret friends, often meeting at that same spot by the river to talk and later..." He trailed off.

A surge of heat flushed Christian's cheeks. That the rabbi had known his mother, talked with her, laughed with her; that *a Jew* had been her friend when Christian had not a single memory of her... His fists clenched. "*You killed her!*"

He expected the man to deny it, but the rabbi lowered his head and nodded. In a small, vanquished voice filled with shame and regret, he said, "I did."

The admission shocked Christian. Choking on his own words, his fingernails scoring his palms, he said in a croaking whisper, "You...you gave her a disease? As grandfather claims?"

Rabbi Yaspha looked up, surprised. "A disease? No!" His confusion transformed into recognition and then into sadness. "No," he said. "I gave her you."

A breeze from off the river dried the sweat from Christian's brow. He shivered.

"It was something not intended, but where Magda led, I followed, helpless. It was something between Jew and Christian that could not be. At least, then. Perhaps not even in this new world the *Korrespondenzausschüsse* are imposing in the Rhineland." Rabbi Yashpha's eyebrows drew together. "But it was right. And good. You. Your being born, your living, is right. You are a child of love. I killed Magda—but she died not by my hand."

Not by his hand? "Grandfather?" he whispered. The thought chilled Christian, rooted him to the earth. And then the second thought nearly stilled his heart. Then, under his breath, so softly, as quiet as a thought, that the rabbi could not hear, "*I* am 'the Jewish disease.'"

Rabbi Yashpha nodded. "Your grandfather would have killed me as well, but your mother refused to give him my name. That she let slip or knowingly taunted your grandfather with the truth, that she cared for—*loved*—a Jew, I would not doubt..." He shook his head, cheeks glistening with tears. He seemed to contract as he wept.

From afar, the bells of the Wormser Dom rang the noon hour, calling the faithful to prayer, but the muffled roar of the crowd at the first of the executions suggested the bells called in vain.

Rabbi Yashpha abruptly stepped forward and hugged Christian. As the rabbi's beard pressed his cheek, Christian smelled the sweat of the Jew's fear and shame but also that of soap and baked bread. The man pulled away. He gazed at Christian. Hesitantly, he extended his hand toward the bloody bandage that bound the remnant of Christian's left ear. Soiled by his labor, the hand trembled. Rabbi Yashpha lowered it and picked up a haversack and a leather pouch that bulged with coins and thrust both into Christian's arms. He then passed him a letter addressed to a J. Curiel of Hamburg.

"Take these, Christian, and go. There is salve and clean bandages inside. Food and water as well. Seek Dom Duarte Nunes da Costa of Hamburg and ask for 'Yaakov.' Quickly now. They'll be coming." He raised his hand in benediction and rested two fingers on Christian's head. "*'Yivarecha Adonai v'yis'm'recha...* May God bless you and keep you. May His face shine upon you and be gracious to you.'" Turning, he placed his shoulders beneath the arms of the cart, lifted, and trudged back between the gravestones toward the road, the cart wheels squeaking.

Christian, his body still rigid, watched him. That every moment of his life had been one of uncertainty, shame, and guilt for reasons he could never guess or know; that his mother had been fearless, inquisitive, brash, courageous, and unaccepting of ignorance and bigotry—like the *Korrespondenzausschüsse* militias; that she had been loving, joyful, and kind...

And his father...a kind man, a loving man, who at least thrice to Christian's knowledge—*Had there been other times?*—intervened to keep Christian from harm.

What would it have been like? To have been cared for, to expect the caress of a hand rather than the back of one, to greet each day with anticipation instead of fear...

To have been looked after instead of looked down upon as...as a disease!

"Your mother died of a Jewish disease!"

Christian's heart raced. He trembled and then shook vigorously as with a violent ague as he watched the diminutive rabbi walk away.

Again.

"I *hate* you!" he shouted at Rabbi Yashpha's back.

The Jew stopped as if struck, then set the wagon down. When he turned, Christian saw tears glistening in the Jew's eyes.

"I know," Rabbi Yashpha said. "I do as well."

Then, like an ox to the yoke, he took up the handles of the corpse cart and shuffled away, back to the city.

Christian watched him until he disappeared from view and then even longer until he could no longer hear the squeaking of the cart's wheels. He was alone amid the silent gravestones and the open trench of unsanctified corpses, all silent save for the buzzing of flies. Then the wind changed direction, coming cool off the Rhine, blowing the stench and flies away. He lowered his face onto the haversack and blinked away tears—then pulled back, startled. Leaning closer, he sniffed deeply, inhaling the scent of lavender that suffused the satchel. Slowly exhaling, he shouldered the pack and set off away from Worms, away from its red stone, curling smoke, and the faint muffled cheers and coarse laughter of the living over the newly dead.

* * *

Omenträger literally means omen bearers but it's used for spies or scouts. That makes Fuchs and his *Omenträger* the fox and his scouts, a deliberate pun by the author.

The Fuchs mentioned in this story is another of the five historical branches of the Fuchs von Bimbach family, the villain from *1634: The Ram Rebellion*. This branch lived in Bischofsheim, across the Rhine River from Mainz. See Dick, Wolfgang R.: Hans Philip Fuchs von Bimbach (ca. 1567– 1626), Patron of Simon Marius. In: Hans Gaab, Pierre Leich (eds.), Simon Marius and His Research. Cham: Springer Nature, 2019, p. 139–177.

The State Library Papers
1632 Non-Fiction

Flint's Shards, Inc.

Buzz! Beekeeping in the 1632 Universe, Part I

Iver P. Cooper

H oney is the oldest sweetener; there is an eight thousand-year-old rock painting in Spain that shows someone climbing a tree to gather honey from a bee hive. By ancient Egyptian times, humans had learned to manage honey bee hives to ensure a reliable supply of honey and beeswax.

In this article, we will explore both how bees were managed by down-timers prior to the Ring of Fire and what the up-timers in Grantville can contribute to the art of beekeeping.

Down-Time European Literature

Several of the ancients (Aristotle, Virgil, Gaius Julius Hyginus, Marcus Terentius Varro, Lucius Junius Columella) wrote about bees and beekeeping. The first English language manual was Thomas Hill's *A Profitable Instruction of the Perfect Ordering of Bees* (1568, 1579), based primarily on classical teachings. Then came Edmund Southerne, *A Treatise Concerning the Right Use and Ordering of Bees* (1593), Charles Butler, *The Feminine Monarchie* (1609, 1623, 1634), and John Levett, *The Ordering of Bees* (1634) with more original writing. Much of what they say about bee biology is wrong, of course.

Beekeeping in Grantville

The Up-Timer Grid does not list anyone as having "beekeeping" as a pre-Ring of Fire occupation, and only one—Daphne (Kinney) Pridmore (1973–)—as having beekeeping as a hobby. She left her job as a clerk at Bargain General to do full-time beekeeping, selling honey, immediately after the Ring of Fire. She was canonized in "A Taste of Home" (Racciato, *Grantville Gazette* 6), but it just briefly refers first to her bees staying snug in their hives while it was raining, and then to the Pridmores having "a contract for supplying honey and mead." There is no description of the hives or her beekeeping methods.

In Appendix 1, I discuss the possibility of additional up-timers who are hobbyist beekeepers. In Appendix 2, I review known and potential "Grantville Literature" on beekeeping.

Western (European) Honey Bees

The honey bees we are most familiar with are the western honey bees, *Apis mellifera*. They originated in Africa and spread naturally to Europe. European colonists introduced them to the New World and Australia. There are almost thirty different subspecies (races, breeds). The most important subspecies are the German (European) black (dark) (*Apis mellifera mellifera*), the Italian (*Apis mellifera ligustica*), the Carniolan (*carnica*), and the Caucasian (*caucasica*) bees (Wilson-Rich 31).

While the German breed was the first one brought to the American colonies, American beekeepers imported other breeds. Italian bees were introduced in 1859 and as of 2004 were the most popular breed in the United States (PennState 19). A queen of one breed could mate with drones of another, so genetic mixing occurred. Wild bees living near Ithaca, New York, in 1977 predominantly exhibited *ligustica* and *carnica* genetic markers, followed by *mellifera* and *caucasica* (Seeley 11).

There are also bred hybrids sold in the United States, notably the Buckfast, Cordovan, and Russian. The subspecies vary in terms of aggressiveness, honey production, swarming tendency, temperature preference, disease resistance, etc.

The Africanized honey bee (*Apis mellifera scutellata*) was created by deliberate breeding. The goal was to "combine the African honeybee's prolific breeding and warm-weather adaptations with the European honeybee's production of honey." Unfortunately, they are quick to attack and persistent in pursuit, and this had not been bred out of them when they were accidentally released into the wild in South America in 1957. They then migrated northward. As of 2000, they had only reached the southern United States (Nosowitz). They would not be found in West Virginia and therefore there is no chance they will bedevil the 1632 universe (unless some idiot decides to breed them).

Bee Life Cycle

The colony consists of three castes of bees: the fertile queen, the male drones, and the infertile female workers. The queen's purpose is to lay eggs and to release pheromones that inform the workers that she is healthy and hard at work. Queens lay the greatest number of eggs in the spring and early summer. During peak production, queens may lay "up to 1,500 eggs per day" (PennState 3). While a queen can live "up to five years," the average productive life span is "2 to 3 years," and some modern beekeepers deliberately replace the queen each year.

For the workers, the development time from egg to adult is 21 days. An adult worker bee lives for four to six weeks in summer, but as much as seven months if it is hatched in the fall (Buchmann 9).

The workers have different tasks, depending partly on age and partly on environmental cues. Young workers are nurse bees; they clean cells and tend the brood. Middle-aged workers convert nectar into honey, build comb, control hive temperature, and guard the entrance. Elderly workers (23+ days old) forage for nectar (Wilson-Rich 78).

Egg-laying begins in late December or early January, but the extent depends on the pollen store. In early spring, the bees begin foraging for nectar, pollen, and water. "The minimum temperature for honeybee flight is 54º F. The optimum temperature for flight activity is 72-77º F, but activity continues up to about 100º F before declining" (UMaine). Foraging activity also decreases with increasing wind speed or decreasing light level. Honey bees stay home if it's raining (UMaine).

The foraging distance is determined by the spatial distribution of nectar sources, and this can change from year to year, and even month to month as flowers bloom and wither. Competition may also be a factor. Beekman reported that the mean foraging distance was 5.5 kilometers. "Only 10% of the bees foraged within 0.5 km of the hive whereas 50% went more than 6 km, 25% more than 7.5 km and 10% more than 9.5 km from the hive" (buzzaboutbees).

The population peaks (perhaps 60,000 worker bees) in early summer and then the hive concentrates on collecting nectar and pollen and storing honey for the winter. To keep warm in winter, bees form a ball, and produce heat by flexing their wing muscles. This of course requires energy that they get from metabolizing honey. Bees start clustering when the ambient temperature drops to 13.9° C. At 20° C, less than 50% are clustered; at 15, 80%; and at 10, 99%. Somewhat surprisingly, Blacquiere says energy consumption at 3° C was 2.6 mg/bee/day, versus 6 at 13.5° C. But Wilson-Rich (74) says that for every 6° C drop in temperature, bees "have to work twice as hard to keep warm and function."

* * *

When the queen's production of pheromones declines with age, the workers prepare "supersedure" cells, from which new (superseding) queens will emerge. A queenless colony can create an emergency queen if the hive contains nurse bees with eggs previously laid by a mated queen, and pollen and honey are available.

When the hive becomes overcrowded, the old queen increases drone laying and the worker bees develop a new queen. When she is ready to emerge, the bees swarm—the old queen and about three-quarters (Seeley 176) of the bees leave and cluster somewhere, usually on the limb of a tree. Scouts find a location for a new home and the swarm builds a new hive. A week later, the new queen goes on a mating flight. In West Virginia, swarming of wild bees is most common from March to June (MAAREC).

There may be more than one swarm. The first one, with the old queen, is the prime swarm and the later ones, with virgin queens, are afterswarms. The later in the season a swarm emerges, the less its chance of survival.

Drones, who eat three times as much food as workers, are "generally present only during late spring and summer," numbering perhaps a few hundred. The drones that mate with the new queen die immediately, and the "also-rans" are forced out in the fall (unless the hive has become queenless) (PennState 3-5).

* * *

Sometimes an entire colony of bees absconds, that is, completely abandons its hive. Absconding is apparently prompted by stressful environmental conditions: high or low temperatures; high humidity; high winds; poor ventilation or drainage; flight path obstruction; a prolonged, severe shortage of nectar sources or water; frequent disturbance; severe invasion by predators or parasites. Absconding is more common in some species and subspecies than others.

Effect of the Ring of Fire

The Ring of Fire occurred on April 2, 2000, and moved Grantville to Thuringia, May 31, 1631. Thus, Daphne's bees lost about two months of time for brood rearing, foraging, and comb and honey production. Grantville moved from the location of Mannington (39.5309° N) to one near Schwarza (50.6186° N) and Rudolstadt (50.7183° N). And it moved from the modern warm climate to the Little Ice Age, albeit not the coldest part of it.

That said, an expert beekeeper (fox41, Graham Stables) advised me that Daphne's hives should be fine. They should hit peak brood production shortly before or shortly after the Ring of Fire. And the bees will arrive "right in the middle of the main European summer meadow crop which should give them a bumper crop if they are on the edge of the ring. Those at the center of the ring will just make do with their normal foraging." He also was of the opinion that Germany in the 1600s would still be warmer than where his hives are located (Aberdeen, Scotland).

He also notes that Daphne's bees will have a numerical advantage. They live in "a tower block" (Langstroth hive) rather than a "cottage" (Damp Skep hive), see below, and if they are inclined to rob the indigenous bee hives the latter will be in trouble.

Hive Design

Clay Pot and Mud Hives

In ancient Egypt and even the modern Middle East, long horizontal tube hives were constructed using clay or mud (Patterson).

Tree and Log Hives

Forest beekeeping was common in northeastern Europe (eastern Germany, Poland, the Baltic and Russia) in medieval times, and indeed it survives to the present day in the Bashkir Urals (Seeley 66ff). Wild bees often nest in tree hollows and German forest beekeepers (*zeidlerei*) found it more profitable in the long run to cut a small hole in the tree, to access the honey periodically, than to cut the tree down. A door or board was placed over the hole and the tree was marked. Ladders or hoists might be needed to access the nest (Kritzky 22-3). In mid-nineteenth century Russia, harvesting was typically no more than thirteen pounds of honeycomb per tree, per year, thus sustainable (Seeley 69).

"In Bavaria forest beekeeping is recorded as early as the year 959 in the vicinity of Grabenstätt." Honey, from hives in the Nürnberg Reichswald, was used to make gingerbread, and in nearby Feucht, there is a castle Zeidlerschloss (Wikipedia/Honey Hunting). Keeping bees in hives cut in living trees is still practiced in Bashkortostan, Russia (Seeley 7).

The next development was the hollowed-out log hive, which could be placed in a more convenient location. Log hives could be set vertically or horizontally, and could be quite elaborate (in the nineteenth century, there were hives with observation windows or movable frames) (Kritzky 24-29). Unfortunately, log hives were heavy, and the log might be better used to make boards.

Skep (Inverted Basket) Hives

Skep hives are commonplace in down-time northwestern Europe (western Germany, the Netherlands, Britain, Ireland and France). They may be made of wicker (braided plant materials), typically with a dung-and-mud mortar, or of straw twisted into coils. Levett, in *The Ordering of Bees* (1634), and Butler, in *The Feminine Monarchie* (1634), both favored straw skeps.

In Europe, skeps were made by specialists (skeppers). The traditional shape was a dome, but in the eighteenth century, flat-topped skeps were introduced.

Another eighteenth-century development was the extension, a straw cylinder placed on top (supering) or below (nadiring). The use of multiple nadirs on the same hive was called "storying." The point of extension was to relieve population pressure and thus discourage swarming (Kritzky 30ff).

Straw is not an especially durable material, and the skep hives were protected by covering them with hackles (conical thatch covers) or (later) cracked milk pans, or by placing them in a bee shelter. Ideally this is a "roofed structure left open on the sides" (Kritzky 54), but there are many old garden walls and buildings with niches for hives.

Skeps were still in use for capturing swarms and transporting bees in the twentieth century (128).

Box Hives

A simple rectangular wooden box hive is depicted in a woodcut from Gallo's *Le venti giornate dell'agricoltura e dei piaceri della villa* (1575) (Getty Images).

The "barrel hive" is an obvious expedient for beekeepers in a port town. The earliest reference I have seen to one was from the nineteenth century, but wooden stave barrels with bulging centers were in extensive use at the time of the Ring of Fire. Some nineteenth-century hives were made using cheese boxes (Kritzky 143).

In 1649, Mews invented the octagonal box hive, the shape approximating a circle—in winter, bees cluster in a spherical mass to conserve heat. His hive was also made of glass rather than wood, thus permitting observation of the bees. Wren (1655) instead used a wooden hive with a glass window in one panel, and added an opening, with a pivoting lid, in the bottom of each box, thus forming a storied hive if the boxes were stacked. The idea could be extended to having an opening in the top of the box as well, as in Janscha's late eighteenth-century rectangular wood box hives (Kritzky 64ff).

An alternative to expanding hives by stacking is by constructing box hives with side openings, so the bees travel from box to box horizontally. This is called a collateral hive, and dates back to late seventeenth-century Italy (73).

While straw skeps were probably used to transport bees to the American colonies, once there, the bees were usually kept in log or box hives (Kritzky 79), wood being in plentiful supply.

The Top Bar and the Movable Frame

In ancient Greece, clay pots with a truncated cone shape were used to keep bees. But there was an important innovation that didn't spread to western Europe until many centuries later: the top bar. This was a wooden rod that rested on the rim of the top opening, and from which a slat of wood was suspended. The bees would use this slat as a foundation for building the comb, and the comb could be lifted out by the top bar (Kritzky 105). Because the pot sides were angled outward, the bees would not attach the comb to the sides of the pot. Vietnamese beekeepers independently developed the top bar concept, applying it to log hives (107).

In western Europe, "the oldest known written references to top-bar hives were in the travel memoirs of Spon (1678) and Wheler (1682), who jointly observed similarly shaped top bar hives—in the form of baskets rather than clay pots—in 1676, in a monastery on Mount Hymettus. (The clay pots remained in use, as is known from a 1696 Cretan memoir.) (Harissis).

It should be noted that while these combs were movable, they were not interchangeable, as the top bars were arranged as parallel chords of a circle, and thus of different lengths.

There have been modern attempts, in Africa, to overcome this deficiency while retaining the sloping side design. Basically, the hive took the form of a trough, with a rectangular top opening, and "straight" or "rounded" trapezoidal short ends (Crane).

While bees could construct comb directly off a top bar, there was greater uniformity if a comb foundation were supplied. EB11 describes the construction of sheets, first of wax and later of metal, "impressed with the hexagonal form of the bee cell." Modern foundations are made of plastic or beeswax (Pennstate). Wires may be embedded to help the foundation resist the stress imposed by a honey extractor.

To more rigidly hold the foundation, side bars and a bottom bar could be added to the top bar, thus forming a frame, typically made of wood. The top bar rests on interior ledges of the hive body, so the frame hangs freely.

The Langstroth Hive

EB11 credits Langstroth with discovering (1851) that the spacing of elements within the hive body was critical. If it was too small (under one-quarter inch), the bees would seal the gap with propolis. If it were too large (over three-eighths inch), the space would be filled with more comb. Either way, the frame would be rendered immovable (Skinner). Unfortunately, EB11 did not state those critical dimensions for "bee space"!

While Daphne Pridmore undoubtedly has some beginner books on beekeeping, I have looked at several, and I would say that fewer than half quantify the required bee space. However, if she bought commercial hive bodies, she can measure the spacing. And if she built her own, she presumably found instructions that provided this information.

The recommended spacing typically falls in the range of 1/4- to 3/8-inch (Skinner; PennState 82). Coleman notes that a gap of 6 mm "is the smallest gap that bees will leave between adjacent comb surfaces" and one of 9 mm "is the usual space the bees will leave between adjacent areas of capped brood. This allows two layers of bees to work back to back...." Also, the gap between the bottom of the frames and the floor beneath it is less critical, "as the bees consider it a similar situation to a wild nest in a cave," and are less likely to build comb there.

Daphne almost certainly uses hives of the Langstroth type. The standard hive body (19.75 x 14.625 inch footprint) holds ten frames, but she might have resorted to a homemade eight-frame model. There are also four depths available: full (9.625 inches high), medium (6.625), shallow (5.0625), and section comb (4.625). A ten-frame full-depth hive body, filled with honey, would weigh over sixty pounds (PennState 7).

The concept of bee space may of course be applied to a top bar hive as well as to a movable frame hive.

Warré's

"People's Hive"

This is a pure "top bar" hive, with no frame or foundation provided. Warré (41, 50) considers comb that is not attached to a framed foundation to be fixed, but this is misleading. Later he refers to use of the hive tool to "lift the top-bars when the honey is harvested" (60).

Miscellaneous

In cold climates, insulation (tar paper, straw) may be added to the outside of the hive (Pennstate 33).

Elevating the hive reduces dampness inside, reduces vulnerability to small ground predators, and makes it easier to inspect and service the hive. But Warré (46ff) objects to elevation greater than 150 mm, saying that it increases exposure to "variations in temperature and to gusts of wind," and that heavily laden foragers may "miss the entrance of the hive and fall on the ground," climbing up to it only with difficulty.

In making sure that the bees have enough honey to survive the winter, the amount of honey in the honey super must be estimated. The traditional way of doing this is by hefting: lift one side and judge the weight. It takes experience, of course. Alternatively, one may actually weigh the super—perhaps with a spring balance—and then subtract the initial weight of the super and the estimated weight of the bees and comb (Heaf).

A single Langstroth hive box, if full of honey, may weigh as much as eighty pounds and there may be a market for a lifting device. Ideally, these are also capable of transporting the hive a short distance (Gouzias).

Apiaries

Wild hives are typically widely separated. A recent study of the Hainrich forest in Thuringia, in which only wild hives exist, reported 0.34 hives per square mile, but depending on the environment, wild hive density might be ten times that (Seeley 41).

The density of hives in modern apiaries is limited by two factors, neighbors and competition. Regarding neighbors, the West Virginia Honey Bee Best Management Practices—adopted post-Ring of Fire—limit the number of colonies to 8 for a 1+ acre lot, 6 for a ½-1 acre lot, and 4 for a smaller lot, with no limit on the number of hives if they are at least 200 feet from the property line. Regarding competition, USDA recommends 1-3 acres of forage per colony of bees. Of course, the greater the distance between the land of one beekeeper and that of the next, the more hives they can put on their land. Mountain Sweet Honey Company reports that it has 75 hives on five acres (mshadmin).

Given that there are 640 acres per square mile, it is plain that managed hive density can be extremely high. This is obviously convenient for the beekeeper. However, it makes it easier for diseases and pests to spread from one hive to another, and also may encourage "robbing."

Bee Crops

The honey bee is a major plant pollinator. But beyond that, it has another advantage: it produces honey and beeswax.

Honey

The bees gather nectar from flowers and sometimes honeydew from certain insects. Open cells in the honeycomb are filled with the nectar. The water content of the nectar is reduced through evaporation by wing fanning; bee enzymes convert most of the sucrose in the nectar and honeydew into fructose and glucose—the honey sugars (EB2002CD/Honey; Buchmann 18ff). The honey-filled cells are sealed with a thin layer of wax ("cap"). If the cell is being used as a brood cell, there will also be an egg inside.

A hive body whose comb contains brood is called a brood chamber, and one that doesn't is called a super. A queen excluder is used to keep the queen from leaving the brood chamber and entering the super to lay eggs. It is a mesh small enough to block the queen but large enough to admit the workers; in Europe, the spacing is typically 4.3 mm (Cushman). It must be removed before winter so the bees can form a cluster.

Honey is a supersaturated solution of the honey sugars. It is about 38% fructose, 31% glucose, 7% maltose, 1% sucrose, 1% other disaccharides, 4% higher carbohydrates, and 17% water (loveridge), but the percentages vary depending on the nectar source.

Honey gradually crystallizes, as glucose comes out of solution. Honey can absorb more water, and if it does, yeasts in the honey can cause fermentation, producing first alcohol and then vinegar. The yeasts can be killed by heat (PennState 70), and fermentation may also be inhibited by cold (71).

A skep hive might produce an average of 20-25 pounds of honey per year. In contrast, a top early twentieth-century hive could produce 200 pounds (EB11).

The beekeeper cannot harvest all of the honey produced unless the bees are being killed; a typical colony needs some honey, probably forty to ninety pounds, to survive the winter (and how much depends on the length and severity of the winter) (Burlew).

Statistics on honey production unfortunately are vague as to whether they are reporting hive gross productivity or beekeeper harvest. The U.S. Honey Industry Report for 2017 indicated a national average "yield" of 55.3 pounds per colony; the West Virginia average was 40. The highest state average was for Hawaii (131) (Flotum). In Britain in 2018, the average "crop" was just over 30 pounds (BBA). In Canada in 2017, the national "production" average was 121.43 (Statistics Canada).

Hive productivity can vary widely depending on hive placement, weather, diseases and pests, beekeeper skill and attentiveness, and competition. An anonymous survey in the Skagit Valley reported that the average amount each beekeeper harvested from his or her harvested hives was 5-62 pounds per hive, with an average just over 29. Brookfield Farm took an average of 18 pounds, but the amount harvested from individual hives ranged from zero to nearly 80 (the keeper left 70 pounds for each full hive) (Brookfield Farm).

Not only is it important to leave the bees enough honey to survive the winter, the honey must be properly distributed. "Most of the [retained] honey should be located above the cluster because the bees will move upward during the winter as they consume their stores" (PennState 32).

Beeswax

Beeswax is a "complex mixture (more than 300 components) of hydrocarbons, free fatty acids, esters of fatty acids and fatty alcohol, diesters and exogenous substances" (Fratini). It has been used to make candles, document seals, figurines, and ear plugs, and as an adhesive, casting material (the "lost wax" process), preservative, engraving resist, preservative, cosmetic emollient and emulsifier, lubricant, rust inhibitor, varnish and polish ingredient. Pharmaceuticals may be dissolved or encapsulated in wax, and thereby slowly released (Bogdanov).

Other Honey Bee Crops

Bee pollen ("bread") is packed and enzymatically treated flower pollen, gathered by foraging worker bees. It is a protein source for the bees. Pollen may be collected using a pollen trap. This fits over the hive entrance and forces returning bees to crawl through a mesh with holes small enough (Cushman recommends 5 mm) that some of the pollen is knocked off.

Propolis ("bee glue") is a natural resinous sealant, made from bee saliva, beeswax, and plant saps. It may be chipped off the hive interior.

Royal jelly is a mixture of proteins, sugars, and fatty acids secreted by nurse bees to nourish queen larvae. To collect it, a colony will be manipulated to develop a large number of queen cells, and the queen larvae removed (and the royal jelly harvested).

Bee venom is a mixture of melittin and other cytotoxic or hemotoxic peptides. It is collected in a manner similar to collecting snake venom.

* * *

Health claims have been made for all of these products, but the evidence is weak.

The Honey and Beeswax Trade

In the Catholic Church, the patron saints of beekeepers include Saint Valentine, Saint Ambrose, Saint Bartholomew, Saint Bernard of Clairvaux, Saint Benedict, and Saint Gobnait. In medieval times, it was not unusual for monasteries to keep hives.

In the Nürnberger Reichwald there was a guild of forest beekeepers as early as 1296. Two other early guilds were the Beekeepers' Union in Zelem, now in Belgium (1486), and the Beekeepers' Guild of Osterhout, near Breda, Netherlands, "started in a small way by the priest of St. John's church" (Crane 447).

The Domesday Book records the number of beehives on demesne land in the counties of Norfolk (421), Suffolk (350), and Essex (599) just after the Norman Conquest (Allsop). The hives on tenant farmer land weren't counted.

In London, there is a Worshipful Company of Wax Chandlers. There was already a company in 1199 but it did not receive a royal charter until 1483. Its biggest concern was cracking down on the adulteration of beeswax with resin, tallow, turpentine, etc., but it also kept an eye on the honey trade. Containers of both beeswax and honey had to be labeled with the maker's mark, and it was illegal to omit the mark or to counterfeit another's mark (Crane).

Posthumus provides old timeline price data from the Amsterdam commodity exchange. In June 1631 (the Ring of Fire was May 31), native honey sold for 26.50 guilders per tun (41.5 gallons; one gallon honey is about twelve pounds). The price was similar in 1632, but jumped to 46.50

in February 1633. By February 1634 it was 51.50. In 1635-36, it was about 37 guilders a tun. Bordeaux honey was 213 (!) guilders in June 1631; 297 four years later. In contrast, Brazilian white sugar was 0.68 guilders per pound in June 1631, and subsequently ranged from 0.70 in early 1633 to 0.58 in March 1636.

Native wax was sold for 67.50 per 100 pound lot in June 1631. The price was 74.50 in May 1633. It peaked at 79 in February 1634, and ran 70-78 guilders in 1635. Baltic (dry) wax was 65.75 in June 1631, and it ran 68-76.50 in 1635-36.

Honey was the chief ingredient of Nürnberg's *lebkuchen* (Strauss 9).

Honey Harvesting

With skep hives, it was necessary to destroy the hives in order to harvest the honey. Sometimes, the bees were killed first. Southerne describes "placing the hive over lit brimstone matches." This would generate poisonous sulfur dioxide gas. A problem with this method, as Butler notes, is that "the honey will smell of the smoke." One may instead "drown them in a tub of water, but that hurteth the honey, and...many of the bees being not quite dead, will sting them that handle the honey."

"Another way to take the combs," Butler says, "is by driving the bees," that is, forcing them to enter another skep first. The occupied hive was inverted and an empty one placed over it. A mantle was wrapped around the junction and tied with a cord. The occupied hive was then struck repeatedly ("drummed") to force the bees (which have a natural tendency to fly upward) into the new skep. A trick not mentioned by Butler is introducing a little smoke into the hive, to force the bees away from the entrance before the inversion (Kritzky 42).

However, driving the bees to a new skep might be just a temporary reprieve. If it occurred in late summer, and the bees were not fed by the keeper, they might starve over the winter (Seeley 72). Butler admitted, "the most usual...manner of taking the combs is by killing the bees." Usually, it was the least and most productive hives that fell victim; the least productive on the theory that they wouldn't survive the winter anyway, and the most productive because they yielded the most honey and wax (Ebert 36).

In the following spring, one needed to multiply the bees rapidly to maintain honey production. Consequently the skep hives were small (9-36 liters), compared to 42 liters for a single ten-frame Langstroth hive body (Seeley 70).

During the Enlightenment, there was an outcry against bee killing. The Society for the Encouragement of Arts, Manufactures and Commerce offered five pounds to each of the first forty claimants who "harvested at least ten pounds of wax in 1767 without killing their bees or letting them starve during the winter." Wildman argued in 1768 that "suffocating bees equated to killing a hen for eggs, murdering a cow for milk, or butchering sheep for wool" (36). Thorley made a more religious argument: bees engaged in "virtuous industry" and did not deserve to be burnt with brimstone. White went a step further, arguing that humanity did not have an uncontrollable right of life and death over divine creation, and killing bees was wanton cruelty (Ebert 36ff). (It will be interesting to see whether there is any crusade against inhumane beekeeping in the 1632 universe.)

The Langstroth hive allowed honeycomb to be removed without destroying the hive or forcing out the bees, as well as being stackable, increasing the potential honey production from a single hive.

* * *

There's still the issue of separating the bees from the honeycomb. Shaking the frame over the hive dislodges most of the bees, and the diehards can be brushed off with a feather. But some beekeepers prefer sterner methods. These include escape boards, fume boards, and blowers. The escape board is placed underneath the honey super and has holes arranged so it is easy for bees to find their way downward and difficult to return. The fume board goes on top of the honey super and has a fabric impregnated with a bee repellent, such as bitter almond.

* * *

Once harvested, the honeycomb could be sold as is ("comb honey") or the honey could be removed from the comb. Prior to the Hruska extractor, this involved "cutting the comb from the frames, crushing it, and straining the honey from the wax. This was both time-consuming and costly..." (Horn 122).

In 1865, Hruska proposed separating liquid honey from comb by centrifugal force. The most advanced form of extractor described by EB11 was the "four frame Cowan." It had four cages for holding combs; the cages were spun up; and the cages were then reversed and spun up again to empty the opposite sides of the combs.

The empty combs may be returned to the hive. This has the advantage of conserving honey supplies, as the bees require a lot of honey (six to eight pounds according to beeswaxco, almost twenty, says Buchmann 4) to make one pound of wax (beeswaxco). However, there is a risk that they carry pests, such as the wax moth or the small hive beetle, or chemicals used to fight those pests.

Bee Veils and Suits

Beekeepers have covered themselves up to protect against bee stings since Roman times. However, the first reference to a suit specifically designed for that purpose was from the eighteenth century.

The most important area to protect was the face, and here the problem was achieving protection without loss of vision. Keys (1796) advocated a veil made of bolting cloth, which was used to sift flour, but dimpled inward, allowing the bees to sting through the openings. Wire mesh (like a fencer's mask), also used in the late eighteenth century, would not dimple inward. However, they were not suitable for hot climates as the metal would heat up and the face could sunburn. Neighbor (1878) pioneered the use of black netting.

Smokers

A smoker is depicted in EB11 but there is no written explanation of the design, other than to say that smoke from smoldering fuel is blown into the hive.

The ability of smoke to pacify bees was well known in ancient times, and the down-timers could read about it in Pliny and Virgil. Hill suggested burning dung. Other fuels used over the years have included dry grass, wood pellets, pine needles, straw, cotton, burlap, cardboard, and tobacco. A fuel that burns slowly and produces a relatively cool, non-toxic smoke is best. Sawdust, synthetic and treated fibers, and petroleum products are undesirable.

The most primitive method of smoking used torches. It was still practiced "until recently in certain regions of Greece" (Harissis 36-37). However, there is a danger of burning the bees, the hive, or the beekeeper, and the smoke is not efficiently directed.

The next step up was the smoking pot. In its most primitive form, it had an open top, and the smoke was blown toward the bees. But there was a danger that dazed bees would fall into the pot. A more advanced pot had a closed top, and both an opening for the beekeeper to blow into, to force out the smoke, and a nozzle from which the smoke would emerge. It also had smaller side openings to supply air for combustion (Harissis 36–37). The seventeenth-century beekeeper could use a tobacco pipe as a miniature smoking pot.

Quinby (1873) is often credited as the first beekeeper to blow smoke into the hive using a bellows; however, this is not accurate. Cotton (1842) depicts a bellows attached by a tube to a skep hive (Kritzky 177). Quinby's improvement was to miniaturize the system by placing "the bellows alongside the fuel chamber."

Daphne certainly owns a smoker, and this can be reverse-engineered. Do-it-yourselfers have made their own smokers (antagonizer).

Swarm Management

While Daphne could buy "package bees" produced by beekeepers in the southern United States or California, down-time beekeepers had to get started by collecting a swarm. A swarm may settle on a tree limb, shrub, or building. Hill (1579) assumes that they are on the branch of a tree and says to "gently saw that off, and lay it on the ground," setting up a hive nearby. Another technique was to place a skep, concave up, beneath the swarm and shake the branch. If one anticipated that a swarm was about to emerge from a hive, one could place a swarm catcher—"a tube of netting held in place by several hoops"—over the entrance (Seeley 70).

Modern apiarists generally endeavor to discourage their own hived bees from swarming, as "colonies that swarm rarely recover in time to produce a significant honey crop" (PennState 27). They control the population density by adding "supers" (enlarging the hive) or dividing the bees (moving a portion to a new, prepared hive). They also destroy "swarm cells" (new queen cells created in anticipation of swarming).

Feeding

A colony should have at least 60 pounds honey for winter food by late fall (PennState 32). If a hive is too light, the bees may be running out of food. "An established colony should have at least 15–20 pounds of honey or the equivalent of three to four full-depth combs of honey in reserve at all times." If the honey store falls below that level, feeding may be desirable. "The need to feed bees occurs mostly in late winter/early spring and sometimes in the fall" (PennState 35).

An alternative to providing sucrose syrup is to provide "inverted" sucrose syrup—this is actually a mixture of glucose and fructose, made by heating the sucrose in water, preferably in the presence of a catalyst (lemon juice, cream of tartar, etc.). The advantage is that the energy cost to the bees is reduced.

But feeding has its dangers. If feeding the bees honey, it should be honey taken previously from the same hive, so as not to run the risk of introducing a new disease. Feeding them cane sugar (sucrose) syrup stresses the bees, as they have "problems inverting the sucrose and handling the excess water" (PennState 25). (The syrup usually has a higher water content than honey.)

Getting the food to the bees is also tricky, as they cannot safely "break cluster" if the weather is cold. The bees will usually be clustered in the top of the hive and so a top feeder has an advantage. A feeder outside the entrance may attract "robber" bees from other hives.

Feeding must begin when it is still warm enough for the bees to convert the syrup to honey. Once clustering begins, it is too late to provide syrup.

In the new timeline, an additional problem is that cane sugar is a luxury item. Indeed, one of the attractions of raising bees is to make honey, a cheaper sweetener. Perhaps one could look at syrup made from plants rich in glucose or fructose. However, "syrups with a predominance of glucose over fructose content pose a potential risk of crystallization in honeybee combs during winter" (Szczesna).

While the starch in grains can be malted, maltose is not a major component of honey and therefore bees may have trouble digesting it. If it is hydrolyzed into the component glucose units, the crystallization risk appears.

Indoor Wintering

In areas with long, harsh winters, some beekeepers have brought their hives indoors. The practice dates back at least to 1868. It allows the bees to break cluster to access supplied food. It is best if the temperature is still one at which the bees are dormant, so they don't produce brood and don't consume the honey stores rapidly. There must be good ventilation to supply adequate levels of oxygen and control levels of carbon dioxide. Some research is directed to finding a level of carbon dioxide that kills mites and not bees.

Wild Hive Hunting

Perhaps you want to raid a wild hive for honey. Or you want to engage in forest beekeeping. Or you plan to force bees out of a wild hive and move them to an artificial hive.

The first step, obviously, is to find the hive. While people speak of bees making a "bee line" home, following them is easier said than done. Some tricks of the trade are in Edgell, *The Bee Hunter* (1948). Set up a two-chambered bait box in a large clearing with lots of flowers. Capture some bees in one chamber, then place comb filled with sugar syrup in the other, and let the bees move to the comb and escape. They load up, fly home, then come back for more. After several round trips they will be making a true "bee line." Mark a few bees with paint, determine their direction of flight with a compass, and estimate the distance by their round trip time. Move the bait box in that direction and repeat the process until the hive is found(Seeley 28ff). Regrettably, these techniques can also be used to steal bees from a managed hive.

Evicting Bees

Sometimes wild bees take up residence in a place where they are a nuisance to people or domestic animals, and a beekeeper will be paid to remove them. There are two basic methods of doing this without harming them. In a trap-out, all entrances but one are closed off and then a mesh cone is placed over the remaining entrance. The bees can fly out but not return. Or, at least that's the theory. It takes weeks. The other is a "forced abscond"; essentially, they are driven out by blowing smoke and bee repellent into a hole drilled into the part of the hive containing the honey (GVB).

Breeding

There is a long history of agriculturalists breeding animals to select for favorable traits (from the agriculturalists' point of view) and against unfavorable ones. This is tricky with bees, because the animals are small and much is hidden within the hive.

A method is needed to observe and quantify the trait of interest. This is usually much easier with a movable frame (or top bar) hive. And it must be possible to raise queens (and drones) from the hives that show the desirable trait.

Having found a queen likely to have favorable genetics, the next problem is controlling who she mates with. Typically, a queen will make one mating flight, perhaps 1.2-1.9 miles from home, and mate with an average of ten to twenty drones at a "drone congregation area." The drones travel even farther averaging 3-4.2 miles (Seeley 178ff). A single drone congregation area might contain "10,000 to 25,000 drones from 200 to 300 colonies of diverse genetic sources" (Bee-Health).

The first solution was to place the queen's hive and the selected drones' hive in a remote area (an island or an isolated mountain valley) to reduce mating diversity. That sounds pretty crude, but in 1935, colonies resistant to American Foulbrood were collected and in 1936 an apiary with just queens and drones from those colonies was established in a somewhat isolated area of Texas. The percentage of colonies with this resistance climbed from 28% in 1935 to almost 75% in 1937. In 1939 it was over 90% (Seeley 87ff).

Complete control is achieved by "instrumental insemination": semen is collected from the drone with a syringe and the queen is anesthetized (with carbon dioxide) and inseminated (under a microscope with a "cold" light). Both inbreeding and outbreeding are possible. The technique even allows mating a single drone to multiple queens, which cannot happen in nature. Instrumental insemination was first demonstrated in 1926 (Cobey) but was not reliable until the 1940s (Seeley 87).

Eastern (Asian) Honey Bee

This bee (*Apis cerana*) is found in central and eastern Asia and has been domesticated. Eight subspecies were recognized in 1999. It was deliberately transplanted to Papua New Guinea in the 1970s and has spread to the Solomon Islands and northeastern Australia. It is very docile and does not make propolis (bee glue). Compared to *Apis mellifera*, its foraging day is longer and its foraging range smaller, which are advantages for targeted crop pollination. It will also forage at colder temperatures. It forms smaller colonies (about 34,000 bees), and its honey and beeswax production is smaller, but that also means that a hive needs less feeding during dearth periods (winter and the rainy season). It is more likely to swarm or abscond (UFIFAS; Partap)

* * *

In China, the second-century scholar Jiang Qi is said to have lived on the outskirts of society, "managing bees." In the following century, Zhang Hua said that in the mountains, swarms were lured to wooden boxes. By the thirteenth century, there were cylindrical, mud-sealed basketwork skep hives, and also "small houses" (box hives?) for bees. Song Xu (circa 1500) described a stacked box hive. Finally, Song Yingxing (a minor character in *1637: The China Venture*), in his 1637 encyclopedia, asserts that "only one-fifth of honey came from kept bees" and that "bees are kept everywhere except in the sugar-growing areas and that 50 percent of the honey produced across the empire comes from the northwest" (Pattinson).

* * *

In Korea, beekeeping began at least two thousand years ago (Kohsaka). In the tenth century, Buddhist monks started to raise their own bees and used the "temple honey" for ritual purposes (Crane 272). Nowadays, the native honey bee "is mostly kept in log hives in the deep mountains" (Jung). The hive stands on a flat stone and is "covered with an inverted porcelain dish" and, in summer, also a straw cover. "After 3-5 years the bees were killed during the winter season, and the honey separated from the combs" (Crane).

* * *

The *Nihon Shoki* (720) chronicle of ancient Japan says that Ambassador Yoho from Baekje (Korea) "let four hives of honeybees loose on Mount Miwa"—this may have been a form of fortune-telling (Crane 273). The Engishiki (905-927) records that honey was given as tribute to the Japanese emperor from Kai, Sagami, Shinano, Noto, Echigo, Bicchu, and Bingo provinces, although the amounts were small, so I doubt they were from managed hives. "Towards the end of the Heian period (794-1185), the "Kon Kagami" describes how bees were kept by the nobility, and the "Konjaku Monogatari" describes how bees were kept by the common people." (Slow Food; BJ).

Beekeeping became more popular in the Edo Period (1603-1868), although it is difficult to judge where it stood in the 1630s. Ekiken Kaibara's *Yamato honzo* (1709), a guide to medicinal herbs, distinguished among rock (mountain), tree, ground, and house honey, and indicated that honey was then produced "in Ise, Kumano in Kii, Owari, Tosa, and" elsewhere. The first detailed description of Japanese bee husbandry was by Kuze Atsuyuki (1791).

"Traditional" (antiquity unknown) vertical hollow log hives (*hatto* or *hachido*, bee cave) may be found on Tsushima Island. Cryptomeria or cypress wood is used. The logs are cut to a height of about 70 centimeters and bored to a diameter of 22–23 centimeters. A swarm is captured in a nectar-baited net hanging from a tree branch, and carried to the log hive. Honey is harvested once a year, from the top of the hive, after smoking the bees (Shimamura). Horizontal log hives were used in Japan at least as early as 1872 (Crane).

An illustration in *Nihon Sankai Meibutsu Zue* (1799) shows simple box and barrel hives, and people reaching into several of the barrels and pulling out honeycomb (Kohsaka). Another, from the Honey Catalogue (1873), shows stacked box hives (Matsuzawa). Bear in mind that Commodore Perry opened Japan to trade in 1854 and that, even before then, the Japanese were getting scientific and economic advice from the Dutch. So these hive designs might not be indigenous and even if they are, might not date back to 1631.

There is an 1811 illustration of a "horizontal cylindrical hive made by binding plant stems together" (Crane). That doesn't correspond to any European design.

Heaf describes a "traditional" Japanese hive design that it considers to be "Warré-like." The source, Syouichi Morimoto, claimed that the system was used in Japan during the "Edo period, 1586-1911" [*recte* 1603-1868]. It is a box hive in which each honey super has a pair of spales forming a horizontal "X" between the corners of the hive (a variant has them as a "+" between the walls). I would not call these spales top bars because they do not actually lie at the top of the comb. The combs formed on these cross pieces are fixed, and the bees are drummed down from the honey super when the keeper is ready to harvest the honey.

There is no way to tell whether the box hives depicted in the historical sources have these spales. An innovation introduced in the early twentieth century would by now be considered "traditional."

* * *

There are many references to honey in ancient Indian texts, but that doesn't mean that bees were managed. A nineteenth-century report indicates that the only place south of the Punjab Himalaya to practice beekeeping was Kanara. There, an earthen pot was prepared for occupation by bees and if they formed a hive, then when the honey was harvested, care was taken not to disturb the brood comb. In the Punjab, beekeeping was common "in the Murree hills, in the tahsil of Rawalpindi, in Hazara, in the Simla hills, and in Kulu" (Watt 267).

The wall hive is a traditional hive design in the Himalayas. It is a "cavity left in a wall when a house is constructed.... It has an entrance on the outside for the bees and is closed on the inside usually with a plank of wood plastered with mud." The cavity becomes the hive and thus differs functionally from the bee niches I discussed elsewhere. In recent times, wall hives have been modernized by removing their combs, transferring each comb to a wire gauze mounted on a frame, etc. (Verma).

Other True Honey Bees

The giant honey bee (*Apis dorsata*) is found from India to southeast Asia. It builds its single comb nest, perhaps four feet wide, in the open, usually high up on trees or cliffs, and therefore it cannot be domesticated in the same way as *Apis mellifera* and *cerana*. The comb is protected by a living curtain of up to 100,000 worker bees. Maximum honey storage is 3-5 kg. Nests are clustered together in communal nest sites of 20-100 colonies. The bees forage at temperatures of 16-40° C, and migrate seasonally between high elevations in the dry season and low elevations in the rainy season. In southeast Asia, particularly Vietnam, traditional beekeepers have a technique for persuading the bees to build their nests on rafters, at least in areas with low vegetation (submerged forests) (Tan; Wilson-Rich 182; UFIFAS; Robinson; Sihag).

It is even more aggressive in the defense of its nest than the Africanized honey bee, so honey hunters seek out its honey on a moonless night, without use of flashlights, so the bees cannot see them. Once at the nest height, which can be over a hundred feet up, the hunters distract the bees with falling sparks from liana torches. The combs are then cut out and brought down (Buchmann 93ff).

* * *

The dwarf honey bee (*Apis florea*) has a similar range. It hasn't been domesticated, either. While a nest will typically contain just 500-1000 grams of honey, *Apis florea* nests are still a target for honey hunters. It's a docile bee, and it forages at temperatures of 18-43° C, which is broader than the range for *mellifera*. Its only common pest is the wax moth (Akratanakul; Sihag).

Meliponines

The "stingless" meliponines are found in the tropics and subtropics of both the eastern and western hemispheres. They are significant pollinators, but only a few species produce enough honey to have attracted human interest.

In the Yucatan and Central America, the Maya made use of *Melipona beecheii*, kept in *jobones* (horizontally stacked hollow log hives). These in turn may be kept in a bee house (*meliponario*) with a palm-thatched roof and open walls. Each hive produces just 3.1-9.3 pounds of honey annually. The honey was used in Mayan rituals and as a medicine (Bratman; Villanueva-Gutiérrez; Buchmann 54-58). In Brazil, the Kayapó manage nine different species of stingless bees (Souza).

Bee Predators, Parasites, and Diseases

Quite a few vertebrate animals are insectivores, and bees can be targets. Bees are staple foods for the bee-eater birds of Africa, Asia, and southern Europe. While these catch the workers on the wing, skunks, bears, and honey badgers attack the hive itself, for the bees, the honey, or both.

Mice are squatters. During fall and winter, they try to build nests inside hives, chewing away comb to make room (PennState 32).

Several insects can trouble a hive. Wasps and hornets kill bees. Hornets are the greater threat as they are both larger than wasps, and are social insects (wasps may be social or solitary). The Asian Giant Hornet ("murder" hornet) is the world's largest hornet and when a scout finds a hive it leaves pheromone markers to attract its nest mates. A single hornet can kill forty bees a minute. However, Japanese honey bees have evolved a "mobbing" defense that effectively cooks a scout hornet to death, and Vietnamese honey bees apparently apply spots of animal feces to the front of the hive as a deterrent.

The small hive beetle is native to sub-Saharan Africa. It appeared in the United States in 1996, but it was not reported in West Virginia until 2003, after the Ring of Fire. It has not been seen in Europe. It will feed on honey, pollen, and bee brood (Neumann; Ellis).

Bees from one hive may attempt to rob another of honey. These robbers can be inhibited by reducing the size of the besieged hive's entrance.

There are two species of wax moth, the greater and lesser. The moth "destroys hives by laying larvae that destroy honeycombs by boring through the wax in search of food" (Horn 294). Pliny speaks of the moth that "devours the wax" (*Natural History*, chapter 21). Hill (1579) refers to a "butterfly" [sic] that "spoyleth the waxe" (cap. xj). They may also attack stored honeycomb. Wax moth damage to stored honey can be prevented by freezing and hives may be protected with para-dichlorobenzene (PennState 57). This is a relatively easy chemical to synthesize: react benzene (from coal tar) and chlorine gas (from electrolysis of sodium chloride) over a Lewis acid catalyst (e.g., ferric chloride), and fractionate the product as needed.

American Foulbrood and European Foulbrood are bacterial diseases, disseminated by spores. They both affect the brood (bee larvae and pupae) and give the hive a foul odor. The spores can survive for seventy years in combs and honey. They are highly resistant to heat, desiccation, and chemical disinfectants.

EB11 speculates that "foul brood" is the disease that Pliny (chapter 20) called *blapsigonia*. He identified it as one which causes the bees to "fail to rear their young." The disease may also have been observed by Southerne, who refers to smelling a "very strong savor issuing out of the hives" (Kritzky 41). While characteristic, the absence of the odor does not mean that the hive is free of foul brood (PennState2011, 31).

The usual way of dealing with a hive that displays symptoms of AFB or EFB is to burn the infected hive and treat nearby hives with the antibiotics sulfathiazole (AFB only) and terramycin (although these will not kill spores) (EB2002CD).

Sulfathiazole is a sulfonamide antibiotic and has been synthesized in undergraduate chemistry classes. It is a likely early target of the 1632 universe chemical industry as it has some efficacy against bubonic plague. See "Infectious Pestilence, Part 2: Fighting the Plague After the Ring of Fire," Cooper, (*Grantville Gazette* 51).

Terramycin (oxytetracycline) has a rather complex chemical structure. It is produced by *Streptomyces rimosus*, which was found in a soil sample in 1950. Unless we are lucky enough to find a producing organism it is unlikely to be available in the new timeline 1630s, as it has a chemical structure too complex to be a candidate for chemical synthesis in that period.

The *Varroa* mite feeds on bee larvae and damages young bees. Its original host was *Apis cerana* but it adapted to *Apis mellifera* when that was brought to Asia (vanEngelsdorp). Thus, *Varroa* is now two species, *Varroa jacobsoni* and *Varroa destructor*. It is not a major problem for *Apis cerana* because that species has a hygienic behavior that effectively limits the infestation to drone brood. In contrast, in *Apis mellifera*, it will reproduce in worker brood. It came to the United States from Asia in 1987 (Horn 293; Roth). If there are beehives in Grantville, they will have it.

The tracheal mite (*Acarapis woodi*) parasitizes the tracheae of young adult bees, interfering with respiration. "Colonies with greater than 40% infection frequently die over winter in the US and Canada."

"Isle of Wight disease," which virtually wiped out the British honey bee population in 1901-1905, was ascribed in 1921 to the tracheal mite. (But in the 1950s, it was reattributed to chronic bee paralysis virus, Wilson-Rich 188.) Still, the early 1900s was when the tracheal mite was first described in Europe (APISIRC), so I would assume that it is not in down-time hives.

The tracheal mite reached the United States in 1984. According to the November 27, 2004, "About" page for the WVBA, in the fall of 2000 the "WVBA invested in breeder queens with a demonstrated resistance to tracheal mites." That strongly suggests that by April 2000, tracheal mites had already reached Grantville. In 2000, about 20% of bee samples (nationwide) submitted to USDA tested positive (Moore). Tracheal mites could spread from Daphne's hives to other hives as a result of drifting (infected bees entering the wrong hive).

Buckfast, Russian, and Carniolan bees have been shown to have tracheal mite resistance (Danka), and it is conceivable that some of Daphne's bees are of those races (although the Russian bees, a relatively new breed, only came to the United States from the Primorsky Krai region in 1997). Of these, only the Carniolan bees are available down-time.

Infected hives may be treated with miticides, but these also have the potential to kill bees (and may be toxic to humans), and mites can develop resistance to them. Synthetic miticides include the pyrethroid fluvalinate and the organophosphate coumaphos (PennState 50). Naturally occurring miticides include the essential oils menthol, eucalyptol, camphor, and formic acid (93). These will be available, with some effort, in the new timeline.

Infection of *Apis cerana* (Asian honey bee) by tracheal mites was first reported in India in 1957 and in Japan in 2009. It has been speculated that tracheal mites were transferred to *Apis cerana* as a result of the importation of *Apis mellifera* (Kojima).

Nosema is a protozoan that invades the digestive tract of adult bees. There are two species, *N. apis* and *N. cerana*, targeting western and eastern honey bees, respectively. EB2002CD says it can be somewhat controlled with fumagillin. Fumagillin was isolated in 1949 from *Aspergillus fumigatus*. Its chemical structure is in the Merck Index but I doubt that a chemical synthesis plan is described in Grantville literature. It was first synthesized in 1972.

Colony Collapse Disorder was first reported in 2006. It has been hypothesized that it results from an interaction between neonicotinoid pesticides and the protozoan *Nosema*.

A continuing concern with the use of pesticides and pharmaceuticals is the possibility of contaminating the honey or beeswax.

Honey Hunting

For those who want honey, but without the trouble of managing a hive, there is honey hunting—following wild bees back to their hive and robbing them of their honey, just like a bear might.

The peak development of this practice might be in sub-Saharan Africa, which is the home of a family of birds known as honeyguides (*Indicatoridae*). The greater honeyguide will deliberately attract humans' attention and lead them to the hive, for them to break it open. The humans take the honey and the bird feeds on the larvae and wax.

News and New Books
Available Now and Coming Soon

Flint's Shards, Inc.

Available Now

Security Solutions, Security Threats, Missions of Security, A Matter of Security, An Angel Called Peterbilt, A Diogenes Club for the Czar

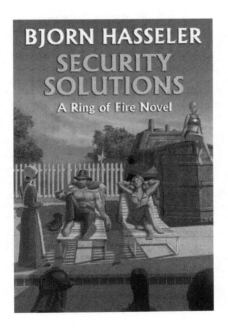

Security Solutions
Bjorn Hasseler

When the Ring of Fire drags Grantville, West Virginia, back to seventeenth-century Germany, down-time veteran Edgar Neustatter finds himself among the survivors of a unit devastated by the up-time Americans and their Swedish allies. Soon, he establishes a new agency: Neustatter's European Security Services.

Security Solutions is the fourth book in the NESS series, after *A Matter of Security, Missions of Security,* and *Security Threats.*

Available here:

https://www.baen.com/security-solutions.html

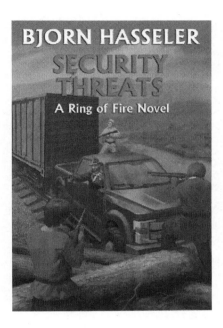

Security Threats
Bjorn Hasseler

Neustatter's European Security Services encounters a campaign of industrial sabotage, a pastor who attempts to limit their client base, an espionage ring, and the aftermath of the Dreeson assassination. Old nemeses and new allies complicate matters.

Somewhere in Grantville is a missing heiress. There's also a Resistance, and it has cookies. Even repeat business with established clients is complicated, not to mention dangerous. Real life proves more complicated than Neustatter's movies or Astrid's books as NESS looks for common threads. Which incidents are related and which are not?

For Astrid Schäubin, solving cases, directing operations, and even portraying a saint are one thing, but figuring out dating in the midst of everything that's happening is quite another.

Security Threats is the third book in the NESS series, after *A Matter of Security* and *Missions of Security*.

Available here:

https://www.baen.com/security-threats.html

"Security Threats" by Bjorn Hasseler

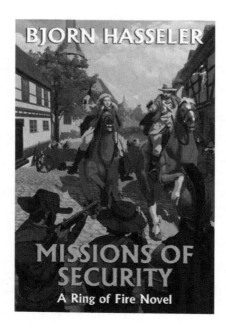

Missions of Security
Bjorn Hasseler

Neustatter's European Security Services is open for business, and business is . . . *too* good?

With the National Guard, private industry, and even a seemingly tranquil farming village caught in an explosive political crossroads all relying on NESS for missions of security, Neustatter and Astrid find themselves pressed to staff, train, and equip the agency while keeping up with their clients' growing requirements in scope and complexity.

-- A simple railway escort mission involves a secretive manufacturing client from Grantville bearing mysterious cargo and a captured fugitive all destined for Magdeburg during the Baltic War . . . what could possibly go wrong?

-- The Bible Society hires NESS to guard a flock of Anabaptist, Catholic, and Lutheran high schoolers *en route* to riot-torn Erfurt and Jena, but will NESS's own pastor tear them apart first?

-- Already strapped for personnel, the last thing Neustatter needs is for a regiment of dragoon militia to choose their wagon train for . . . "involuntary provisioning." Can a handful of badly outnumbered agents protect a village that isn't sure it wants their help?

Missions of Security is the sequel to *A Matter of Security*, and contains the full text of the previously published short story, "Blood in Erfurt.

Available here:

https://www.baen.com/missions-of-security.html

"Missions of Security" by Bjorn Hasseler

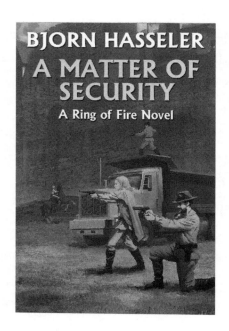

A Matter of Security
Bjorn Hasseler

It's a matter of security. When the Ring of Fire drags Grantville, West Virginia, back to seventeenth-century Germany, down-time veteran Edgar Neustatter finds himself among the survivors of a unit devastated by the up-time Americans and their Swedish allies. After wintering in Grantville, they return home to find that while they have changed, their village has not. Having glimpsed the promise of a republic ruled by its people rather than lords and tyrants, Neustatter leads his men and their families back to Grantville to establish a new agency: Neustatter's European Security Services.

The city from the future counts cowboys and detectives among its heroes—and still needs them. Join Neustatter, Astrid Schaubin, and NESS as they face desperate refugees, towns on the edge of revolution, and those who want to preserve the old order at all costs, while juggling basic training, modern education, and the day-to-day challenges of living in a boom town. Does NESS have the flexibility, training, and firepower to survive in the new timeline?

This is the first of the 1632 books originally published by Ring of Fire Press to be rereleased as an ebook by Baen Books.

Available here:

https://www.baen.com/a-matter-of-security.html

"A Matter of Security" by Bjorn Hasseler

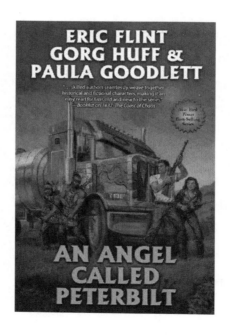

An Angel Called Peterbilt
Eric Flint, Gorg Huff, and Paula Goodlett

HISTORY WILL NEVER BE THE SAME AFTER A PETERBILT TANKER TRUCK FULL OF OIL IS TRANSPORTED BACK ONE THOUSAND YEARS IN TIME. A NEW NOVEL IN ERIC FLINT'S ASSITI SHARDS SERIES BY RING-OF-FIRE STALWARTS GORG HUFF AND PAULA GOODLETT.

Michael and Melanie Anderle are hauling a tanker full of oil with their Peterbilt eighteen-wheeler when they're struck by a temporal irregularity that sends them, the truck, and their daughter back in time a thousand years. The bubble that transports them also grabs a chemist and her two young children, along with half a convenience store in the middle of the United States.

They just want to make a decent life for themselves in this new world of the past, with their Peterbilt and its oil providing a means of transportation, a generator, and shelter. But not all the locals are willing to live and let live, and when the area shamans decide that this community of temporally displaced persons is a threat to their power, the Anderles find out what it's like to take a Peterbilt to war.

Available here:

https://www.baen.com/an-angel-called-peterbilt.html

*"An Angel Called Peterbilt" by
Eric Flint, Gorg Huff, and Paula
Goodlett*

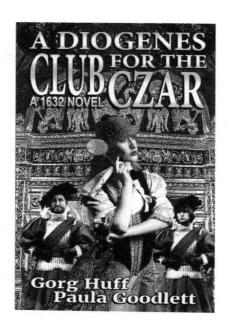

A Diogenes Club For the Czar
Gorg Huff and Paula Goodlett

This is the fourth Miroslava Holmes book and all the Holmes books have dealt with Russian politics, but this one deals with them even more. Events from *1638: The Sovereign States* are included in this novel and from there it continues the story of the main Russian thread of the 1632 Universe.

Czar Mikhail Romanov of the United Sovereign States of Russia has problems by the score.

The Embassy Bureau is run by an incompetent from an important family, who is possibly a traitor. Sheremetev is gone, only to be replaced by Mikhail's Uncle Ivan, who, if he's as corrupt as Sheremetev was, is a lot more competent. The advances in technology mean that while he can defend himself against Muscovite Russia, he doesn't have the forces to defeat them.

So it's looking like a long stalemated war.

Russia can't afford a long war. The Sovereign States has no port not blocked by Muscovite Russia and the Swedes. Even if he should defeat Muscovite Russia, the Polish Lithuanian Commonwealth would still be sitting between him and western Europe. His foreign credit is failing and the conflict between the free states and the serf states is getting ready to shatter his new nation before the ink is dry on his new constitution. The royal chef can't prepare a proper croissant. The *Pravdivyye Fakty* is printing fantasies and code groups that are telling the Muscovites who his agents are, while the only private detective in Russia is off on the far end of Kazak.

Now someone has killed a congressman.

What's a czar to do? Mikhail needs another Grantville. Another Ring of Fire to bring innovations to Russia, enough innovations so that the rich and powerful can't steal all the new wealth before it reaches the poor.

Mikhail doesn't ask for it but he gets what he needs. Because what he needs is *A Diogenes Club for the Czar*.

Coming Soon
Legions of Pestilence, The Trouble with Hugeunots

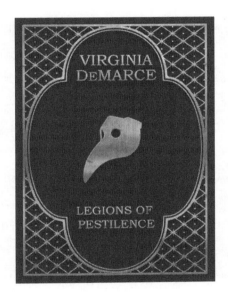

Legions of Pestilence
Virginia DeMarce

"In the world the West Virginians of Grantville came from, the borderlands between France and Germany had been a source of turmoil for centuries. In the new universe created by the Ring of Fire, the situation isn't any better. The chaotic condition of the German lands has been ended--for a time, at least. And the near-century long war between Spain and the Netherlands has finally been resolved.

But now France is unstable. The defeat of Richelieu's forces in the Ostend War has weakened the Red Cardinal's grip on political power and emboldened his enemies, Foremost among them is King Louis XIII's ambitious younger brother, Monsieur Gaston. An inveterate schemer and would-be usurper, Gaston's response to the new conditions in France is to launch a military adventure. He invades the Duchy of Lorraine. Soon, others are drawn into the conflict. The Low Countries ruled by King Ferdinand and Duke Bernhard's newly formed Burgundy, a kingdom-in-all-but-name, send their own troops into Lorraine. Chaos expands and spreads up and down the Rhine.

It isn't long before the mightiest and most deadly army enters the fray--the legions of pestilence. Bubonic plague and typhus lead the way, but others soon follow: dysentery, deadly and disfiguring smallpox, along with new diseases introduced by the time-displaced town of Grantville. The war is on. All the wars--and on all fronts. Can the medical knowledge of the up-time Americans be adapted and spread fast enough to forestall disaster? Or will their advanced military technology simply win one war in order to lose the other and much more terrible one?"

Full book available Tuesday, June 4, 2024

Available here:

https://www.baen.com/legions-of-pestilence.html

Legions of Pestilence

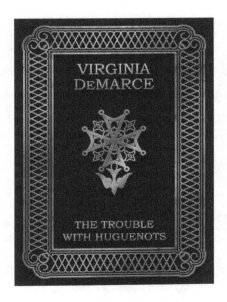

The Trouble with Huguenots
Virginia DeMarce

Ever since the assassination of King Louis XIII and the overthrow of his chief minister, Cardinal Richelieu, France has been in political and military turmoil. The possibility—even the likelihood—of revolution hovers in the background. The new king Gaston, whom many consider an usurper, is no friend of France's Protestants, known as the Huguenots. The fears and hostility of the Huguenots toward the French crown have only been heightened by the knowledge brought back in time by the Americans of the town of Grantville. Half a century in the future, the French king of the time would revoke the Edict of Nantes of 1598, which proclaimed that the rights of Huguenots would be respected. At the center of all this turmoil is the universally recognized leader of the Huguenots: Duke Henri de Rohan. He knows from the same up-time history books that he is "scheduled" to die less than two years in the future and he has pressing problem on his hands. His estranged wife and brother are siding with the usurper Gaston and plotting against him. Still worse, his sole child and heir is his nineteen-year-old daughter Marguerite. He believes he has less than two years to find a suitable husband for her—but acceptable Calvinist noblemen, French or foreign, are sparse at the moment. What's a father to do?

Full book available Tuesday, July 2, 2024

Available in the July 2024 bundle.

https://www.baen.com/the-trouble-with-huguenots-demarce.html

The Trouble with Huguenots

Connect with Eric Flint's 1632 & Beyond

We would love to hear from you here at *Eric Flint's 1632 & Beyond!* There are lots of ways to get in touch with us and we look forward to hearing from you.

Main Sites

Email: 1632Magazine@1632Magazine.com

Shop: 1632Magazine.com

Author Site: Author.1632Magazine.com

For anyone interested in writing in the 1632verse, or fans interested in more background on the series and how we keep track of everything.

Social Media

Our Facebook Group is our primary social media, but we do use the FB Page, YouTube, and Instagram accounts.

Facebook Group: The Grantville Gazette / 1632 & Beyond

YouTube: 1632andBeyond

Facebook Page: Facebook.com/t1632andBeyond

Reviews and More

Because reviews really do matter, especially for small publishers and indie authors, please take a few minutes to post a review online or wherever you find books, and don't forget to tell your friends to check us out!

You are welcome to join us on **BaensBar.net**. Most of the chatting about 1632 on the Bar is in the 1632 Tech forum. If you want to read and comment on possible future stories, check out 1632 Slush (stories) and 1632 Slush Comments on BaensBar.net.

If you are interested in writing in the 1632 universe, that's fabulous! Please visit **Author.1632Magazine.com** (QR code above) for more information.

Made in the USA
Middletown, DE
12 May 2024

54235489R00099